Icy cold bony fingers of unbelievable strength fastened around Joe's neck, tightened and squeezed. His arms flailed but they made no impression on his attacker as he was pulled to the floor, kicking weakly.

From the Dark Hours

Guy N. Smith

SINISTER HORROR COMPANY

PRESENTS

FROM THE DARK HOURS

GUY N. SMITH

From the Dark Hours

Edited by J. R. Park
Cover art by Mike McGee
Cover design by J. R. Park

Published by The Sinister Horror Company

From the Dark Hours -- 1st ed.
ISBN 978-1-912578-32-0

ACKNOWLEDGEMENTS

A special thank you to Shane Agnew for unearthing *The Immortals*.

THE SINISTER CHAMPIONS

Anthony Watson, Chris Hall,
David Lars Chamberlain, Emma Audsley,
Gary Harper, James Steel, Jason Kelly,
Jorge Wiles, Matt Shaw, Paul M. Feeney,
Rebekah Mann, Steve Matthewman,
Thomas Joyce, Tracy Fahey
& Wayne Parkin
Thank you for your support.

To become a Sinister Champion, visit our
Patreon page for details at:

www.patreon.com/SinisterHorrorCompany

*For all the Guy N. Smith fans that help keep his legend
and memory burning brightly.*

Contents

Introduction

Whilst collecting my thoughts to write this introduction it feels strange to think of Guy in the past tense: Guy *was* a prolific writer; Guy *was* a master of pulp fiction across genres, Guy *was* a kind and gracious person.

When we started work on this collection Guy was very much fighting fit. Despite awaiting hip surgery to correct an injury that had slowed his mobility, he was as enthusiastic as ever about his writing and talked excitedly about plans for future releases. He may have been 81, but he was more productive and passionate about his writing than I have seen in people a quarter his age.

Guy N. Smith

I was always amazed at the number of stories he had been working on, from short stories to novels. A lot of his shorts he sold to anthologies, and he liked to keep a reserve of these, writing more as inspiration struck, so when asked by a publisher to purchase a tale of his, he'd have something already prepared.

With the success of *Tales from the Graveyard*, we decided another collection would be worth pursuing, and so Guy raided his files, pulling together some old obscurities that had barely seen the light of day, along with more recent ones.

Reading this collection, you'll be hard pushed to work out which ones are which (unless maybe you refer to Shane P. Agnew's excellent *Guy N Smith Illustrated Bibliography*). And that's one of the things I found amazing about Guy's writing, he never lost his teeth when it came to horror. The stories in this collection are as deviant, foul and brutal as anything he penned across his lengthy career (well except maybe for *Bamboo Guerillas*, but that's on a different level of nasty compared to anything else in his catalogue).

FROM THE DARK HOURS

So here is one of the last projects that myself and Guy worked on. I know he'd be so pleased that you hold it in your hands.

Enjoy the adventures of ghosts, monsters and wild beasts as Guy, once more, guides you through worlds born of shadows; nightmares from the dark hours.

- J. R. Park

Beasts Of The Dark Hours

Of short and powerful build Frank Headbetter had moved from their suburban home in the Midlands to a cottage incorporating ten acres of rough hillside on the Shropshire/ Welsh border. Remote, and with stunning views over the mountains, it was his dream home.

Elaine, his wife, petite with long fair hair, was somewhat dubious of their move. However, she told herself that she would get used to it in time. It was Frank's dream home and there was no way that he would ever move from here. His lottery win last year had completely changed their lives.

Frank was a freelance journalist able to work from home apart from the occasional trip to interview a client. His lifelong hobby was shooting and currently he was working on building up their small acreage into a shoot combined with a nature reserve.

'I could do with a rabbit for the weekend,' Elaine announced over breakfast one morning.

'I'll go out and get one later.' He bit on a slice of toast. 'I want to check the ride down the bottom by the stream. I glimpsed a muntjac down there the other week. Could well be we'll be having some venison in the freezer before long.'

Half an hour later he set out, his 12-bore shotgun under his arm. It was a warm spring morning, a delight to be out whether or not he bagged a rabbit. A couple of pheasants burst out of cover, wood pigeons were in abundance.

Then he was down on the bottom ride which he had neatly strimmed the previous autumn. A winding stream bordered his neighbour's farm, twisting and turning.

It was along here that he came upon animal footprints that were certainly not made by any species of deer. He caught his breath, instantly recognised them from those occasions when he had accompanied a mate down in the Forest of Dean. *Wild boar without a doubt, an adult, undoubtedly accompanied by youngsters, and large ones certainly made by a male. It had been reported in the press that they were spreading out due to extensive culling by the forestry commission. And now some had found their way up here!*

Frank trembled with excitement. If he fed this ride then there was a chance that he might bag the big one, leaving the mother and her young, to mature. They probably lived in the big forest up beyond the narrow lane at the top of his own land. The sooner he began feeding down here, the better.

On the way back he bowled over a rabbit which bolted from the gorse. That would keep Elaine happy. Later on he would return with some potatoes and set up a feeding point for the boar. Life was suddenly very exciting.

That afternoon half a sack of potatoes was placed on the lower ride. Next morning on checking, he found that they had been eaten amidst a surround of boar prints. Male, female and youngsters had found them. In the meantime, he would feed again. Then tomorrow, an hour or so before dark, he would come down with his heavy .308 rifle and wait and watch. If the boar showed up, he would take the big fellow, leave the female and her young.

Strangely this acreage seemed devoid of wildlife that afternoon. No pheasants, no pigeon, no sign of a rabbit, like everything was avoiding those monster newcomers. The very thought sent an icy trickle up his spine.

The following afternoon he went to check that feeding point. He carried his 12-bore shotgun in case an opportunity arose to bag a pigeon or two. If the boar had returned to that feeding point, then towards dusk he would return with his heavy .308 rifle.

The boars had definitely returned to their feeding point, the last of the potatoes were gone and there was a morass of footprints; male, female and youngsters. He trembled with excitement at the thought of his stalk a few hours later.

It was then that he was aware of a heavy rustling in the thick undergrowth on the steep slope above. He froze, watching and waiting.

It was then that the big male boar emerged up ahead, a fearsome creature. Its head was lifted, its small eyes focused on himself.

Doubtless it would return whence it had come. These creatures avoided human contact at all times. At least that had been his experience down in the Forest of Dean. God, if only he had brought the .308 instead of the shotgun this fellow would have been dead meat!

The monster did not return whence it had come. It stood there watching him, a creature of sheer evil.

He backed away. Maybe if he departed now all would be well and it would return at deep dusk.

And then it moved forward, heading towards him and there was no mistaking its intention. It had singled him out as a foe who needed to be gored to death.

As it advanced, Frank gave way to panic. If only he had his heavy rifle... The shotgun came up to his shoulder and in sheer panic he fired both barrels of No. 6 shot at the creature. It splattered the boar, tiny wounds but in no way did it halt its advance.

Frank grabbed the lower branch of a sizable silver birch tree, hauled himself up. The shotgun fell from his grasp, but it would have been of no use against this huge beast. He pulled himself up onto the next branch; now he was safe from any frenzied attack.

The boar halted at the foot of the tree, looked up at its intended prey. It was bleeding from a score of minuscule wounds, but no way had they impeded it. There was no mistaking its sheer rage.

Frank sat astride a heavy bough, prayed that it would not snap beneath his weight. Maybe that bastard would give up and go away before long. Right now it showed no signs of departure. A human had inflicted injuries upon it and he had to pay the price for it.

The long wait showed no signs of ending as the afternoon wore on.

Elaine had heard the double shots. Maybe her husband had bagged her another rabbit or a brace of wood pigeons.

The afternoon drew to a close, dusk was already creeping across the sky. Frank should have been home by now. What the hell had delayed him? A troubled thought crossed her mind. Suppose he had had an accident, was lying out there wounded and bleeding…

There was only one thing for it, she had to go and look for him before darkness closed in.

She let herself in by the roadside gate, began the steep and tricky descent.

'Frank... Frank, where are you?' She paused, waited for a reply.

'Elaine,' it was faint, distant, came from down below. 'Don't come any nearer. Go and get help!'

What the hell had happened?

Elaine almost fell in her haste to answer Frank's call for help. Stumbling, grabbing a bush to spare herself a fall.

'I'm coming Frank.'

'Go back. Fetch Carl, tell him to bring his rifle!'

She ignored her husband's shouts, reached the lower ride. He had to be somewhere along here…

Then she saw him aloft, clinging to a branch which threatened to snap at any second, the wild boar beneath, blood oozing from a multitude of shotgun pellet wounds.

'Oh, God Almighty!'

Seconds past and then the irate wounded creature moved. It stiffened, turned and began loping towards her.

There was nowhere that offered safety from the impending attack. She froze, screamed. Then it was upon her, throwing her onto the ground, a tusk boring into her, gouging between her spread thighs.

Frank lowered himself from his perch, retrieved the fallen shotgun, snapping the breach open, extracting the spent shells and loading two live ones. He ran to where the crazed beast was boring into his wife's genitalia.

Up close, he triggered a charge of shot into the attacker's rear where it was clear of her body. The boar fell back, rolled over. A second close-range shot blew a gaping, bloody hole into its side. It lay motionless, a mass of blood-soaked coarse hair.

'Oh, my poor darling,' Frank leaned over his unconscious wife, vomiting at the sight of her wounds.

That was when he became aware of the undergrowth close by crackling, and a number of wild boars emerged, the female and her four youngsters. They had no fear of the humans, the male had rendered them helpless. They scented flesh ready to be devoured.

Frank's scream was cut short as the big female tore out his throat. The youngsters were quarrelling over the fresh meat on offer, a scrabbling mass of striped fur tearing at strings of flesh, ripping it away from both humans.

Slurping noisily, they fed greedily, cracking bones, splattering fresh blood over themselves and the dead male who had led them to this unprecedented carnage. He, like his victims, had sacrificed his life but that was none of their concern.

Their appetites satisfied, they trailed behind their mother, up through the overgrown hillside and back to the dense forest beyond the narrow lane where they had made their new home.

They had tasted human flesh and from now on they would be seeking more. There were always ramblers in that huge acreage of conifers.

Night Of The Necrophile

Donald walked the back streets of the big city every night, a routine he rarely missed regardless of the weather. Pouring rain or driving snow never deterred him from his obsession which had started some years ago when he was in his twenties.

Tall and handsome with flaxen hair tied up in a ponytail, his coat was buttoned up to the collar for it was a frosty night. Nevertheless, he scarcely noticed the freezing atmosphere as his eyes scanned both pavements. The cold had certainly not deterred a number of women who leaned in darkened doorways and entrances to alleys, glowing cigarettes denoting their presence; prostitutes seeking custom as was always the case here.

He noted in one alleyway a couple embraced, the female with her back to the wall, her jeans and knickers down below her knees. A man was pushing into her, grunting his pleasure aloud.

Donald's erection stiffened still further as he paused momentarily. They had not noticed his presence; they probably would not care if they had. He stood there, straining his eyes into the deep gloom. God, he could have watched all night, for Donald was a voyeur, had been since his boyhood days.

He had only once had a girlfriend, pretty little Janie. She had come from a strict, conventional family and had had it drilled into her that sex before marriage was a sin. She had let him feel her on a couple of occasions, through her panties, of course. No way would she drop them for him, not even for a bit of finger. She got real wet, soaked her underwear and Donald ejaculated in his briefs. But she refused to allow him to expose himself to her. God, it was agony.

Then Janie jilted him, found herself another guy. Christ, within a few months she was pregnant and her folks kicked her out. That was when Donald's problems began and he started mooching the streets at night, drooling over whores. Their approaches were many but he hurried on. For some inexplicable reason he would not oblige or be obliged. His phobia was firmly established. He masturbated every night in his lonely house which he rented, fantasised about how it might have been with Janie, or one of those young slags out there. But somehow his phobia always stopped him. It almost happened on one occasion, an attractive whore had stepped out of the shadows, cigarette glowing between her lips. 'Only a fiver, love. There's a bit of lawn up the back of that house and the folks are away.' Her hand stretched out an intended feel through his trousers just to ensure a paying customer. She even made contact with Donald's throbbing organ - and that was when he turned and fled, coming in his trousers as he ran. God, he had wanked some when he went to bed that night! One night, he tried to convince himself, it would surely happen sometime.

He moved on from his voyeurism that night, passed a scruffy slag who stated that she was "desperate for a dick" and would give him a stand-up job for just a couple of quid. No way!

Then this girl emerged from a passageway between two houses. So beautiful, she could not have been more than twenty, small and slim, a shaft of streetlight revealing features that reminded him of Janie, long dark hair falling about her shoulders. Her blouse was undone in spite of the cold. She wasn't wearing a bra and her slender fingers played with her nipples.

'Hi, there.' A soft, cultured voice so different from the majority of her kind who grunted crude offers. 'I could use some company tonight. I'm lonely.'

He caught his breath, stopped and faced her. His erect tool throbbed, he thought he was going to come.

'I... I,' he swallowed, words would not come.

'I've got a comfy bedsit just up the road,' her smile had him going weak at the knees.

That was when his phobia took over. He grunted something unintelligible, turned on his heel and began to walk away, back the way he had come. He would go back home, lie naked on the bed and wank like fury, fantasising about what might have been.

That was when he heard footsteps behind him, a dainty fast tip-tapping. He glanced round, in the distance a streetlamp revealed that same girl. Christ, she was following him!

Instinctively, he quickened his step, turned into the adjacent street. It was only about five minutes to his house from here; he would lose her, disappear from her view. He did not want to, but he had to, he began to tremble. He could not face a sexual encounter, preferring to fantasize about what might have been in the safety of his own home.

His hand shook as he inserted the key in the lock. That was when he heard female screams some distance away. They ended abruptly. He paused, listening, but the only sounds were those of late-night traffic.

It was not altogether uncommon. On occasions clients treated whores roughly, perhaps a refusal to pay. He glanced up and down the street but there was nobody in sight Ah well, it was none of his business. He entered and that throbbing erection blinded him to all else. He could not wait to undress and lie on the bed.

His tool was bloated like he had never experienced before, pulling the foreskin back was painful, exposing the head in its glistening moistness, warm semen on his slipping fingers. Strewth, and all because of that wench out there! Why the hell hadn't he taken her up on her offer? He could have brought her back here and shagged her at his leisure. She might even have agreed to stay the night.

Brian Walton had lived in this area ever since boyhood. It was okay if you minded your own business, ignored the whores. He had long given up cussing them, most of them knew him by sight anyway and did not even bother making an approach. Mostly he stayed indoors at night with his wife Edna.

Tonight seemed busier than usual out there. He drew the curtains, settled down to watch the telly.

'When are we going to look for somewhere in a more respectable area?' Edna had asked that question many times before. 'It would be nice to live in a street that wasn't infested by whores.'

'One of these days maybe,' he replied, yawned. 'They don't bother us and…'

Outside somebody was screaming, female cries that were suddenly cut off.

'What the hell…'

'You'd better go and take a look, Brian. Sounds like somebody is being murdered.'

He rose from his seat with a sigh, shuffled towards the front door, unlocked it.

He stared across the street, made out a female lying on the pavement, a man in a thick overcoat kneeling over her. Even from here Brian could discern hands encircling her throat, grunting angrily.

'Hey!' he shouted. 'What the hell's going on?'

The attacker leaped to his feet, glanced in Brian's direction and then hurried away. The girl lay there, arms and legs splayed. She did not move.

'God Almighty!' Brian rushed over, knelt down by the prone female, ran his hands over her. She still didn't move, her throat was red and swollen. He felt for her pulse. Nothing. *'Christ, she's dead. That bastard strangled her!'*

He looked up and down the dimly lit street. There was nobody in sight. Any prostitutes which had been hanging around had disappeared. The man who had attacked this lovely girl with long dark hair was no longer in view.

Brian knew that he had to call the police immediately. He staggered back to the house. Edna was waiting in the open doorway.

'Whatever...' She was shaken, trembling.

'There's been a murder,' he grunted as he pushed past her. 'Let me get to the phone.'

A police car arrived, blue lights flashing, within five minutes. Brian stepped out into the street as three uniformed officers alighted.

'Right, where's the body?' one asked tersely.

'Just across there…' Brian's voicer tailed off. He stared up where the car's headlights blazed. *The street was empty, there was no sign of the young whore who had been sprawled on the pavement a few minutes earlier.*

'Making bogus calls is an offence,' one of the policemen snapped.

'I'll show you exactly where she lay.' Brian had a sinking feeling in his stomach as he led the way up the pavement. This was too crazy to be true, that girl had been as dead as the provincial door nail and now she had vanished.

'Right there,' he pointed, stood back. His companions stooped, shone their flashlight.

'That's a spot of blood,' one of them grunted, 'and there's another. She couldn't have been dead, she's gone that way. We'd better follow it up, make some enquiries of the residents. No, we don't need you, Mister Walters. We'll call and talk to you later.'

Brian stood and watched them leave, a trio shining their torches on the concrete, pausing to check every so often. He shrugged his shoulders, it was all beyond belief. He knew without a doubt that the victim of the attack had been stone dead. Right now it was all too much to take in.

Donald grunted his pleasure aloud as he ejaculated, sperm shooting up on to his bare stomach, rubbing his member frantically with slipping fingers. Oh, if only that beautiful whore had been up here on the bed with him. He would have shagged her all night. He let out a sigh of regret. It was too late now but maybe tomorrow night he would go back and try to find her. His penis began to soften but then hardened again. His fingers moved up and down it, warm and slippery.

That was when he heard the click of the front door opening down below. He must have forgotten to latch it when he returned. Somebody had entered his house. Who the hell could it be?

Soft slow footsteps padded up the stairs. They halted outside the bedroom doors, he heard soft breathing. In a moment of panic he pulled the sheet up over his naked body.

The door creaked open, somebody was coming into the bedroom. He tensed and then he saw a slim female figure in the soft glow of the streetlamp which filtered in through the uncurtained window, long dark hair falling across her naked breasts. Her blouse hung in shreds like it had been ripped open. Her slender throat was torn and bruised.

He recalled those earlier screams. Had she torn herself free of a violent client and sought safety with himself, seen him entering his house?

'Hallo, there,' he spoke falteringly. 'Has... has somebody attacked you? You're quite safe here.'

She did not reply, just stood there in the glow from the window, smiling. Her slender hands tore the remnants of her blouse, tossed it away. The nipples on her exposed breasts were stiff and engorged. She unfastened her jeans, let them fall to her ankles, kicked them away. She was not wearing underwear, had doubtless embarked upon her nocturnal outing prepared for action. Now she was stark naked, stepping out of her shoes and reaching for the sheet which hid his own nudity from her sparkling dark eyes.

She did not speak a word, she did not need to as her slim fingers closed over his pulsing penis. Donald groaned softly.

Then in one movement she swung herself onto the bed, lay beside him, her lips meeting with his own. Her grip on his member tightened but she did not rub it, she knew only too well how close to an ejaculation he was.

Her lithe body came upright, kneeling over him, pulling his thighs together, opening her own, guiding his throbbing organ in between and up inside her.

Donald gasped. *She was icy cold, her entire body freezing as though she had just emerged from a refrigerator.* He gasped aloud but it did not impair his pleasure as she moved herself up and down on him.

He ejaculated instantly but his erection did not soften. On and on, her rhythmic movements demanding a second orgasm. Then a third. He was exhausted by that time and only then did she disengage, stretching out by his side, her fingers encircling his penis, stroking it as it softened.

Oh, how cold she was. It must have been the result of hours of soliciting out in that hard frost, he told himself.

He dozed and then he was suddenly jerked fully awake by a loud banging on the front door.

'Police. Open up!'

There was no way he could have freed himself from her freezing embrace. More banging on the door then the sound of heavy footsteps mounting the stairs. The bedroom door was flung back on its hinges, the light was switched on.

Dazzled, Donald saw three uniformed police officers, one holding a taser. They surrounded the bed, two pinning him down, the third examining the unmoving naked form by his side.

'Dead as a dodo!' the latter grunted. 'Strangled. He must've dragged her back here after he attacked her, left a trail of blood spots all the way. Then shagged her until she finally died.'

His companions grimaced. 'We'd better call the paramedics to come and collect the corpse, we'll need a full investigation into the cause of death although it's pretty obvious. As for this guy…' he addressed Donald, 'You'd better get dressed before we take you in. We're arresting you on suspicion of murder, anything you do say may be taken down and used in evidence …'

The Lair Of The Giant Squid

'That's where we'll find it!' There was a near fanatical gleam in Professor Danielson's piercing blue eyes as he stabbed at the wall map with his forefinger as though he bore that particular designated area of ocean a personal grudge. 'Right there, give or take a mile or two. I'd stake my pension on that's where the giant squid is hiding out!'

Kline, the fisherman, who had only flown in from the Great Barrier Reef the previous day, stroked his greying beard doubtfully. 'There's more ocean than land in this world of ours, professor. Me, I wouldn't like to say where he's holed up.'

'You ever seen a giant squid, Klin?' Danielson whirled on the other almost accusingly. He had flown the fisherman here on the advice of an old colleague. Professor Cliff Davenport had told him that Klin knew more about the oceans than all the boffins put together. The trouble was, Cliff had added, Klin kept most of what he knew to himself. But he was a good man to have around if you went down really deep.

'Nobody who's ever seen it has lived to tell the tale,' Klin replied in a matter-of-fact tone. 'Which is one of the reasons why I ain't particularly keen on gettin' a glimpse of it.'

'You were instrumental in ridding the oceans of those giant crabs though. Davenport tells me that you roasted one lot in the mangoes with a swamp fire.'

'I caught 'em on land and that's a whole lot different from fighting 'em down below. That old squid, you'll have to chase him in his own domain.'

'Well, I'd like to get a look at him,' Danielson smiled. 'Next best thing to getting a picture of the Loch Ness monster! I take it you'll come with us, we've got funds to launch an expedition around the Chatham Islands, New Zealand's ocean plateau. The Smithsonian Institute's National Museum of Natural History in Washington are backing us. I'm a teuthologist there, Klin.'

'A what?' Klin never stood on ceremony.

'In layman's terms, a squid expert. Our collection at the Institute numbers over one hundred thousand specimens, the biggest weighs a quarter of a tonne. The only one we don't have is the big one. You got any idea what it looks like, Klin, how big it is?'

'I guess it's a big 'un.'

'It's seventy feet in length, purple in colour and has ten arms full of suckers, and it's eyes are as big as footballs. They've been catching one or two baby ones off the Chatham Islands, about twenty feet long, but every marine scientist would give his right arm for a glimpse of ol' granddaddy.'

'An' probably lose more'n his right arm if he got close to it,' Klin retorted. 'Okay, I'll come along.' He refrained from adding "just for the money." Even Klin knew where to draw the line. 'You'll need sperm whales to track it. Sperm whales go crazy if they get a smell o'squid.'

'We've arranged all that,' Danielson snapped.

'An' you'll need to go real deep to find Big Boy, deeper'n a submarines pressure will stand.'

'We're using an acrylic sub. It'll dive to a depth of three thousand feet comfortably.'

'Sounds like we might be in with a shout, Prof,' which was the nearest Klin ever got to paying anybody a compliment.

'The sperm whales have picked up a scent!' There was no mistaking the excitement in Danielson's voice. 'Just look at 'em go, Klin.'

'Little squids,' Klin grinned. 'Sperm whales ain't particularly interested in the size so long as it's a squid. See, they're hunting 'em out now. The squids have changed colour to blend in with their surroundings but they ain't fooled the whales. Squids are backpedalling,' Klin watched closely. 'That funnel in its head shoots out water, propels it backwards. Now, look, they're releasing a coloured dye to cover their retreat but they won't fool the whales.'

'I *am* a teuthologist, you know!' Danielson snapped.

Simpson and Walters, the other two members of the four-man crew exchanged winks. This expedition had its own comedy show to relieve the boredom but the professor wasn't laughing.

The sperm whales caught and killed, moved on. The submarine followed.

Suddenly, Klin tensed, leaned forward.

'I don't see anything,' Danielson muttered.

'Them sperms,' Klin rarely showed traces of emotion; he did now. 'They're workin' up to a killin' frenzy. More'n just a scent o' tiddlers. Me, I reckon we could be gettin' close!'

The water was churning, it was difficult to make anything out at all. Four pairs of eyes were watching closely. The crew were tense, expectant, maybe they picked it up from Klin. His hunches were seldom wrong.

'There she is!' Klin yelled. 'The Big One!'

The water was cloudy, none of them could make out anything more than a shape. But it was big. Colossal.

'At last!' Professor Danielson breathed. 'I've waited a lifetime for this!'

Klin's eyes narrowed, he curbed his exuberance. The shape was about the size of a cow, smaller than the dimensions Danielson had quoted for a giant squid. Smaller, but infinitely more awesome. There was something threatening about the way it heaved itself off the ocean bed.

'The sperm whales,' the professor's tone was one of dismayed surprise, 'they've taken off, fled! What the hell is going on, they should be going in for the kill.'

'They ain't!' Kiln grunted. 'Because that ain't no squid, no matter how hard you try to make it one. It's... oh, Jesus, there's more of 'em. Dozens of 'em! They've been hiding up here all the time, just when we thought they were...'

'What is it, man?' Danielson shouted.

'Crabs!' The others might have been mistaken but it seemed that there was a note of fear in the big man's voice. 'The Big One, the one we thought we'd exterminated. King Crab, Queen crab, it don't matter which but it's starin' us right in the face and it don't look none too friendly. And it's got all the others down here with it, breedin' and growin' till they're big enough to move inshore and start all over again. Let's get the hell outa here!'

Then they all saw it, instinctively drew back.

'It... they must have killed the Giant Squid, taking over as rulers of the ocean,' Danielson breathed.

'Get the hell out of here!' Klin yelled. 'You guys don't understand what they can do. I've seen 'em tip a tank over, cut into it like it was a can o' meat.'

But it was already too late. Even as the submarine started to surface, something struck it a devastating blow on the side. The wall bulged inward; outside, the water pressure seized on a vulnerable area.

The submarine juddered, those inside had the feeling that a giant crane had clamped it, began to squeeze. The roof buckled. The engine was making no impression, the lift upward had come to an abrupt halt.

'Just my luck,' Klin thrust his face close to the professor's. 'I just got paid big money for gettin' myself killed an' I ain't had time to spend none of it.'

Klin turned back to watch. They were trapped, they had blundered right into the Crab's spawning area. Like Danielson had said, the crustaceans must have killed the Giant Squid and were now the rulers of the deep.

'Well, we ain't goin' nowhere!' Klin laughed. As one who had gambled with life and death all his life, he wasn't complaining. No way was he going to cower to that lot out there.

If he was destined to go, then he'd go down fighting. He reached behind him for a small axe; it was puny. Useless.

But it was a token gesture of his defiance right to the bitter end. There would be no surrender on his part.

The Prison Cell Door

'Surely to God you're not going to buy one of those!' Diana Frost grimaced, stared at the stack of heavy doors in the storeroom below the Dartmoor prison museum.

'Don't worry yourself, love.' Her husband Joe was tall with greying hair, an inveterate collector of whatever took his fancy, which had resulted in their sizable Midlands house resembling a museum. 'One would be fine as a cellar door, far better than that tatty cracked one. You won't see it at the bottom of the steps and in any case, you never go down there, do you?'

'Hmm,' she pursed her lips, shook her head. 'If Joe had made up his mind on purchasing one of those doors then there was nothing she could do except grin and bear it.

'I think I'll take this one,' he struggled to pull one of those doors clear of the others. 'It'll need quite a lot of renovation but once that's done it will be fine. No problem.'

The curator standing behind them spoke for the first time. 'All them doors are made of Columbia pine,' he tapped the one which Joe had pulled clear of the others. 'They date from around 1850 when the prison was rebuilt and became a British Convict venue. Now the prison is being renovated and all new doors will be fitted. As you can see, the locks have been removed from all of them for security purposes. Home Office rules have informed us that none are to be sold with their locks. As it happens a new governor is taking one next month and I've heard that he is going to stop the sale of these doors and they will all be burned. Must say I can't see the reasoning behind it. So you're just in time, Mister Frost. Fifty quid okay with you?'

'Fine,' Joe smiled and his wife turned away. 'My Range Rover is parked outside.'

'In that case I'll give you a lift up with this door.'

The following day Joe dragged the door down the cellar steps, propped it up against the wall. God, it needed some work doing on it, all chipped and scratched, but he relished the prospect. He would buy a new lock from the ironmongery in town. Well, there was no time like the present for making a start.

Sometime later he became aware of something hidden within the stout woodwork. He had to prise it free with a screwdriver.

Jesus, it was a small file!

No way could that tool cut through a steel bar! Its purpose suddenly dawned upon him. It was a weapon, doubtless conceded for the purpose of poking out a warden's eyes!

The complete renovation of that door took him all of four days and then, with a replacement lock fitted, he struggled to hang it in place. It fitted, creaked as it swung on its hinges. Superb, worth every bit of that fifty quid!

In the days following Joe's acquisition of the cell door the subject was not so much mentioned between himself and Diana. She had no reason to go down to the cellar and the door was hidden in the shadow of the rail bordering both sides of the steps. She would try to forget it was there.

That cellar had always been a storage place for things not wanted around the house, rubbish items which someday might be useful. Joe kept his stock of wine in a crate at the far end, ideally cool and the only time he visited that place was to fetch a bottle up for the table. Both he and his wife were lovers of red wine.

It was after this evening meal, a few days following the completion of the door's restoration, that Joe realised they would be needing a bottle for their evening meal on the morrow.

Diana had finished the washing up, they were later than usual due to a shopping trip in town.

'Strewth, I'm shattered,' she yawned. 'In fact, I think I'll have an early night.'

'Fine,' he scraped his chair back, stood up. 'There's football on the telly which I want to watch so I'll join you later.'

'I'll be fast asleep,' she yawned again.

'First, though, I'll go down and fetch a bottle of wine for tomorrow whilst I think about it.'

She nodded. She did not even want to think about that cellar and its dreadful entrance. She headed towards the stairs.

Joe made for the steps down to the cellar. One had to tread carefully for the kitchen light did not penetrate down there.

That was when he discovered that the door was unlocked, which was strange as habitually he kept it locked. After all, what was the point of buying and fitting a new lock if one did not want to use it? He must have overlooked locking it behind him on a previous occasion when he had fetched a bottle. No problem.

The door was unusually stiff on its hinges, he had to push it hard in order to swing it open. Like it was saying "do not enter". That was really stupid.

He reached inside, flicked the light switch. The single bulb flickered, threatened to extinguish before it came on.

For some reason a sense of unease filtered through him, an icy trickle ran up his spine. Don't be bloody stupid, he told himself.

His stock of wine was stored in a wooden packing case in the far corner. All he needed was to cross the uneven floor, grab a bottle and get the hell out of here. And don't forget to lock the door behind you this time!

That was when the light almost extinguished, then came on again. A thud behind him, the door had slammed shut. Strange, there was no breeze blowing down from above. No matter, though, it would not be locked.

He shivered; it was damnably cold in here. Even though the cellar was below ground it should not have been this cold in the midst of a summer heatwave.

He shuffled across the uneven floor, grabbed a bottle of red wine, turned to retrace his steps and that was when the bulb went out. It came back on again almost immediately but this time only to a dim glow, just enough to enable him to make out his surroundings.

Next time I come down I'll bring a replacement bulb, Joe thought. He made it to the door, tugged at it. It would not budge. What the hell, it was impossible for it to have locked itself!

He banged on it with his fist, pulled again, but it would not move. This was impossible.

A shiver ran up his spine. Something made him turn around and stare into the deep shadows.

And that was when he saw the figure crouched in the far corner. It was human, balding with strands of loose hair hanging over the near fleshless features, eyes barely visible in the sunken sockets, wide toothless mouth in what could only be interpreted as a snarl, saliva dripping from the lips on to a ragged hairy chin. The hands were clasped around the knees, skeletal with ragged fingernails. Torn clothing revealed filthy flesh. Joe saw that the torn remnants of a jacket was marked with black arrow heads - once a prison garment doubtless.

Who the hell was this guy and how did he get in here? A nauseating aroma of what could only be decomposing flesh had the bile rising in Joe's throat. His hands shook, released their grip on the bottle of wine. It slipped from his grasp, shattered on the floor.

Now that figure in the corner was struggling to its feet, holding onto the wall for support, advancing unsteadily. Any second it might fall.

It did not. Fleshless hands reached out for Joe Frost and somehow secured an unbelievably strong hold on his jacket.

Foul breath fanned his face, had him spewing.

'They're going to hang me,' cracked words that seemed to come from afar. 'Not now, though. You have rescued me but you must pay the full price for it!'

Icy cold bony fingers of unbelievable strength fastened around Joe's neck, tightened and squeezed. His arms flailed but they made no impression on his attacker as he was pulled to the floor, kicking weakly. Shards of broken glass cut into his body. Blood trickled down his shirt.

He was weakening by the second, his pleas for mercy barely whispers. The bulb had dimmed still further, any second it would extinguish. That was when he blacked out, a victim of this inexplicable being who was strangling him.

A sudden crack on his neck snapped and he did not hear the heavy prison door creaking open, then clicking shut as his murderer shuffled up the steps beyond.

'Joe?' Diana called from the kitchen.

'I'm afraid there's nothing we can do for either of them,' one of the two medics who had answered the call shook his head. 'It has all the hallmarks of a strangling, a vicious murder. We will take them for a diagnosis and see if there is any clue to who killed your neighbours.'

'There was nobody else around when I came to look for them.' Bridget wrung her hands in anguish and disbelief. 'I stopped by as I always do on a Thursday for a game of cards. I'm used to letting myself in, but when there was no one to greet me, I went looking around the house - and found *this!*'

The paramedics wrinkled their noses, the stench in the cellar was overpowering, reminded them of those occasions when they had been called out to a corpse which had been undiscovered for some considerable time.

They loaded up the bodies, which had to go to Porton Down for an investigation into the cause of death, and awaited the arrival of the police.

'Seems like the murderer entered the house, by the look of it, strangled the Frosts and hid their bodies in the cellar,' Chief Inspector Willis addressed two of his officers in his small office. 'A thorough investigation is already taking place. There does not appear to be any motive, in fact some loose cash on the kitchen table had not been stolen. We have no description of the intruder. Strangely the Frosts' CCTV on the front of their house shows nobody except that neighbour who came to check on them. It's inexplicable!'

'But the stink down in that cellar,' Sergeant Wilson wrinkled his nose at the memory, 'it was like those bodies had lain unnoticed for weeks before being discovered, and were decomposing. In all probability the Frosts had only been dead for a couple of days or so at the most.'

'Very odd,' Willis was aware of an icy shudder running up his spine. 'I phoned Dartmoor Prison and they informed me that the door had once been on a cell where prisoners awaiting execution were confined. During the late nineteenth century there had been an escapee, a dangerous murderer. He was never recaptured. Not that I think it has any bearing on these recent murders. That guy would have been long dead by this time!'

THE PRISON CELL DOOR

An uneasy silence followed. Another shiver ran up the inspector's spine and the hand holding a sheet of notes trembled slightly.

The Shrunken Head

'I really do appreciate you coming all the way from Johannesburg just to be with me on my ninetieth birthday,' Frank Shaefer ushered his visitor into the lounge of his small semi-detached house in a north London suburb.

A casual observer might well have put Schaefer's age at around seventy. Tall and sparse, he retained most of his faculties, both physical and mental. His aquiline features were lined, his grey hair was thinning, but his blue eyes had not lost their glint. A raw-boned veteran, he had hunted in both Africa and India up until around twenty years ago.

'I wouldn't have missed your ninetieth for the world,' Bryan Gilligan was in his early sixties, still working for his small hunting agency. Tanned and balding he sported a neat goatee beard. 'After all, Frank, you taught me to hunt and I owe my life to you. I still have nightmares about that day when we tracked that wounded buffalo in the dense bush. When it suddenly charged and I panicked, missed it with both barrels. I wouldn't be here now if you hadn't dropped it stone dead with a single shot, rolled it over barely ten yards in front of me.'

'That's the thrill of big-game hunting,' Schaefer smiled. 'The danger, the adventure.'

They fell silent, sipped sherry, each with their own memories of days long gone. Gilligan's eyes roved his host's collection of memorabilia which filled the room, mounted trophies on the wall, shelves overcrowded with a variety of small trinkets. Frank Schaefer ensured that memories of his past were kept alive now that he was too old to hunt.

Gilligan's roving gaze alighted on an item which clearly had pride of place amongst an array on the upper shelf. A shrunken head, approximately the size of a large, clenched fist, a rare collectible which dated back to the days prior to protection being afforded to those jungle pygmies which had once been fair game for hunters. These days surviving relics fetched sizeable money at auctions. A recent trend was that of models constructed from wood, replicas for those unable or unwilling to purchase an original. Ugh! The very idea revolted him and brought back memories of that day in his youth when he had hunted with Frank on the fringe of that mighty, impenetrable strip of jungle.

'You remember him, then?' Schaefer gave a hollow laugh. 'I've named him Jo-Jo. A special friend from a memorable hunt. Doubtless you remember it?'

Gilligan experienced a sense of revulsion at the memory, the only hunt with his companion which he wished that he could forget. On occasions he had nightmares about it, woke up sweating and switched the light on.

Frank was keen to bag one of the lions which inhabited that place, most of which had long learned to lie low in the dense undergrowth when they winded a hunting party in the vicinity. There was always the chance, though, that one would emerge if a stalk was slow and quiet. Bryan's companion had instructed the porters to remain on the outskirts.

The mid-day heat was stifling. Surely even lions would be glad of the cool shade within that forest. Bryan was convinced that he and Frank were wasting their time, it would have been better to have rested up until later in the day.

Suddenly Schaefer stopped, crouched low. He had spotted something up ahead. A movement and then Bryan glimpsed a small human figure bursting from cover and fleeing at full speed towards the forest, one of the pygmies which resided there, seeking safety from those hunters who had shot numerous of its own kind in days gone by. They had recently been afforded legal protection but the small inhabitants were not to know that.

Schaefer's double .500 Express was lifted to his shoulder. Surely not, Bryan was shocked, for his companion was only too familiar with the hunting laws…

A deafening report followed. Up ahead that running pygmy fell, was hidden from their view.

'Got the little bugger!' A triumphant shout and Schaefer was running forward. Bryan followed, aghast that the other had deliberately flouted the recent protection afforded to these small jungle folk.

The pygmy was floundering in the dense grass, its right leg smashed, almost severed by the heavy bullet. It was whimpering, cursing.

Schaefer lowered his double rifle to the ground, withdrew a heavy hunting knife from a sheath on his belt, advanced on the writhing figure. One hand pinned the latter down, the razor-sharp blade began sawing at its neck, slicing deep. An instant beheading that silenced the screams and curses. Then Frank Schaefer rose to his feet, holding the head of his victim aloft, blood dripping from the severed neck.

Oh, Jesus! Gilligan turned away, vomited.

'I've always wanted one of these,' there was no mistaking the glee in Schaefer's voice. 'That's why I shot the blighter in the leg, didn't want to spoil the head. Now we'll head back to base. As the poet Ghalib once said "it is not the sins I have committed that I regret but those which I have had no opportunity to commit." We'll leave the lions for another day. Kyanga will shrink and cure this head for me, he has done many for hunters over the years. Pay him the right money and he'll keep his mouth shut. Rumour has it that he was once a witch doctor. A creepy sort of guy but he'll do a good job, I've no doubt.'

Even with the passing of the years, memories of that day still brought back revulsion for Bryan Gilligan. Now sitting here in the lounge of an ordinary suburban London house he experienced a feeling of sickness. That shrunken head, its piercing tiny eyes seemed to focus on himself. *You are as guilty as he who did this to me.* With an effort he jerked his gaze away from that revolting "trophy" up there on the shelf.

'I'm pleased I got myself a shrunken head before I left Africa,' Frank Schaefer's voice seemed to come from afar. 'Little feller should be pleased to have such a good home. If he'd remained in that jungle he'd probably have been killed and eaten by lions like many of his kind.'

They retired to the adjoining dining room to eat a dinner cooked by Schaefer; crocodile burgers. 'Bought from the supermarket down the road,' it was a kind of veiled apology. 'Best I could do now that I no longer hunt.'

'They're fine. I've always been fond of croc.'

'Going back to that shrunken head…'

Strewth, can't we forget it and enjoy our meal? It's becoming a sort of hoodoo.

'I think you'll agree Kyanga made an excellent job of it. Just like it still lives. I gave him twenty dollars. Strange remark he made just as I was leaving him. He said that perhaps one day I'd regret shooting that pygmy. I thought maybe he was warning me about being caught at customs trying to bring it back to England. No such misfortune, I'm pleased to say. I wrapped it in a towel and hid it in my suitcase. They never even looked in there.'

'It gives me the creeps,' Bryan grimaced. 'Those eyes… its very expression like it still has life in it and it hates you for what you did to it. Me too, because I was with you when you beheaded it.'

'All in the imagination,' Schaefer gave a laugh but it sounded hollow, forced. 'I can assure you, little Jo-Jo's as dead as the proverbial dodo.'

After they had eaten they retired to the lounge. Bryan found his eyes drawn back to that top shelf much as he tried to resist it, a kind of hypnotic command *"look at me"*.

He stared, stiffened with disbelief. Before dinner that head had been turned towards Frank, now it was facing himself, those tiny eyes staring hatefully. There was no mistaking the sheer malice in them.

'As I was saying at dinner, Bryan…'

'Frank…' his voice shook, the hand which pointed upward trembled, 'it…it's moved whilst we were out of the room, now it's staring straight at me instead of at you!'

Schaefer followed the other's gaze. 'That's certainly odd… maybe we're imagining it. I dusted that shelf only this morning. Could be I didn't put it back quite level. There's one or two mice in this house, I'm trying to trap them. A mouse might have nudged it…' His explanation did not sound very convincing. 'Anyway, it doesn't really matter.'

Both men lapsed into an uneasy silence.

'If you don't mind, I'm going to have an early night,' Gilligan stood up. 'I've had a long tiring day.'

'I'll show you to your room, Bryan. I'll just have another whisky and then I guess I'll be ready for bed, too.'

After his visitor had retired Schaefer poured himself a whisky and relaxed in his chair. It was certainly strange how that stuffed head had changed position. There had to be a logical explanation but right now he was too tired to think of one. He dozed fitfully.

Sometime later he was awakened by a soft thud like something had fallen from his collection of memorabilia on the shelves. His uplifted eyes focused on that top shelf. Where that head should have rested there was an empty gap! Mice again, he clung to the only logical explanation he could think of. It must have been perched precariously and the little buggers had knocked it again.

There was another gap close by. That was where his treasured hunting knife had been displayed, the one which he had used to behead his favourite trophy. This was crazy!

Only then did he become aware of a stealthy padded movement across the floor below, like tiny bare feet shuffling on the frayed carpet. What the hell was going on?

Then he saw it, a human shape no more than three feet in height, shiny black skin, naked except for a loincloth, its right hand grasping his hunting knife, wielding it threateningly. It jabbered in its native tongue but there was no mistaking its anger and threatening dialogue.

Frank Schaefer froze in horror. A pygmy from that dense African jungle was threatening him, no longer just a head but now it had returned to life in its original form. Long dead it had risen.

A single bound took it up onto the arm of the chair, balancing with agility, the knife raised. Schaefer was paralysed with terror. A fleeting explanation crossed his tortured brain. Kyanga the witch doctor was exacting revenge for the beheading of his own kind, his evil magic had lain dormant until now.

A scream was rising but it died to a gurgle as the heavy, sharp blade slashed deep into his throat. Blood spurted as his attacker sawed with unbelievable strength for his small size, cutting through flesh and bone.

Schaefer's head fell from his shoulders, thudded on the floor, rolled across the room. Only then did the blood covered pygmy jump down, wiped the blade on his victim's leg and headed towards the stairs.

Upstairs, sleeping soundly, was the other hunter who had stood by and witnessed that murderous act in a distant land decades ago. Only when he had suffered a similar fate would the pygmy's vengeance be complete.

THE SHRUNKEN HEAD

The pygmy stood by the side of the bed. He offered up his silent thanks to Kyanga whose magic had made it possible for both hunters to pay the supreme price. He thrust the knife deep into Gilligan's carotid artery, the pain woke the hunter instantly. The vision before him was terrifying, he clutched at his throat senses reeling, his brain already starved of oxygen. He died staring into those glinting eyes so full of hatred.

Laughing and cursing in his native tongue the pygmy finished his gruesome task and beheaded Bryan Gilligan.

Days later when the headless corpses were discovered by police following phone calls from concerned neighbours, the shrunken head was back on that shelf covered in dried blood, the hunting knife alongside it.

The Clairvoyant

Mr Theophilus was the most morbid of men. Nobody who lived in the suburban street, where his conventional semi-detached bachelor abode was to be found, could ever remember having seen him smile. He was a total recluse, rarely being seen outside the house except when he drove his car to the office each morning, leaving promptly at 8:30 a.m. and returning each evening shortly before 6 p.m. His dress never varied. He always wore a black, pinstripe suit and a bowler hat, his pale, hatchet-like face reminding one at once of a professional mourner.

He was, naturally, a source of mystery as far as the neighbours were concerned. The city swallowed him up for five days of the week, and for the remaining two he stayed indoors, cleaning and cooking for himself, and allowing the garden to go untended. 'Where does he work?' they asked one another. 'Why does he shut himself in the house on fine weekends? What does he find to do?'

Mr Theophilus found plenty to do, in fact. In the spare bedroom he had a most comprehensive library, incorporating for the most part annuals of the Black Art. A wooden altar, draped with a black cloth stood in the corner opposite the window, with an effigy of the Master himself above it. Strange circles and signs were drawn on the floor and walls and two black candles burned incessantly.

Yet, Mr Theophilus had never attended a Black Mass, or made contact with any of the other covens in the city. He had always been a lone wolf, and even in his worshipping of all that was evil, he was reluctant to share his interests with others. He had no need to, for all that he knew he had taught himself from the books which filled the shelves on the walls of his secret room. And he had succeeded far beyond his wildest dreams.

THE CLAIRVOYANT

John Theophilus was beginning to wish that he had never picked up that book on the Powers of Darkness in that frowsty second-hand bookshop more than ten years ago. A casual, passing interest had led to all this, and now he had a tiger by the tail. He knew that there was no escape for him now. He was hooked for life, as surely as if he were a hardened drug addict on heroin.

The stockbroker's clerk, for that had been his profession for the last thirty years, had meddled and experimented with that which he had learnt from his many books, until one day, quite by accident, he had discovered that most feared gift of all, namely the ability to foresee events in the future. However, nobody more than he regretted that cursed foresight, for he found that, although he knew things were going to happen at a specific time, either to himself or to others, he was quite powerless to alter the course of events in any way whatsoever. He could not look into the future at will, in the manner of a pseudo crystal gazer in a fairground tent. Indeed, he had no means of knowing when information regarding events portending would be conveyed to him. Sometimes he went for months at a time without any advance warning of things to come, and then, suddenly, one morning he would wake up with the knowledge that a certain thing would happen that day. Vividly, he recalled the first instance when it had occurred, possibly five years ago. He knew as he drove to work, that there would be a fire in the warehouse in the street adjacent to his own office. He dismissed it as pure imagination and attempted, unsuccessfully, to push it to the back of his mind. However, when he heard the sirens in the middle of the afternoon, followed shortly afterwards by the clanging of fire engines, clouds of dense black smoke and crowds gathering on the street corner, he knew then that he had been endowed with a gift by his Master, far beyond the normal powers of his fellow mortals.

Three weeks later he again woke with the certainty of an impending catastrophe. The elevator in his own office block would crash to the basement level, three stories below, at lunchtime. Miss Stone, the elderly spinster who worked at the desk opposite, would be one of the five people killed. Still, he consoled himself, as he threaded his way through the early morning traffic, he would warn her or somehow prevent her from entering that cage of death he would alter the hand of Fate.

The morning seemed to drag endlessly on, and he glanced up at the large clock on the wall as he noticed Miss Stone methodically clearing her desk before going to lunch. 12:57! In three minutes she would be dead unless... He wished he could have warned the others, but how could he without arousing unwanted suspicion? If he did so, and nothing happened, everybody would think him mad. If the elevator crashed, as he knew it would, they might accuse him of a premeditated murder of which he had become squeamish at the last minute and tried to call the whole thing off. But at least he could save Miss Stone...

'Miss Stone,' he began already having thought of an excuse, to delay her for those few vital minutes. 'I...'

She was gone! He hadn't seen her leave the room, and yet as he made a panic-stricken dive for the door in a desperate attempt to call her back, he again noticed the hands of the clock. 1 p.m. exactly, they stated. Yet only seconds ago, they had shown at least three minutes to the hour. It was though his own actions had been frozen, unknown to himself, as time marched on.

'Miss Stone,' he yelled at the top of his voice as he burst into the outer corridor. 'Miss Stone, come back!' And then he heard the rending crash from far below, followed by the inevitable screams. He realised then just how powerless he really was.

Daily, after that, he awoke to the terror that the details of one certain future event might be portrayed in his fear crazed brain, namely the time and manner of his own death. He was like a man in a trance now, frequently knowing what would happen at some specific time, and powerless to warn or help those who might be involved. He could have saved the president from assassination once, and yet each time he tried to telephone a warning his fingers were incapable of dialling the number, as though they were paralyzed. He attempted to tell Mr Busby, a trusted friend and colleague, yet the words just would not come out, and he found himself discussing prices of various stocks and shares instead. It was always the same.

At last that terrible day dawned, and as Mr Theophilus shaved, he suddenly realised that today he was going to die. Strangely, he was not given over to panic, but calmly finished his ablutions whilst the terrible knowledge unfolded itself in his brain. It would happen on his return home from the office that evening, on the junction of Barker Street and Wroxton Road. It would be a lorry. He had always dreaded lorries!

Suddenly a determined glint appeared in John Theophilus's eyes. Just who, he asked himself, gazing in proud admiration of his reflection in the shaving mirror, did they think they were dealing with? He prepared and ate his breakfast in his usual calm manner, and then, when he had cleared away the table, he went out to the coal house, and returned with a small axe. Mounting the stairs, he entered his satanic chamber, where, methodically he destroyed everything which related in any way to his Master. The altar was smashed to smithereens, along with the plaster effigy, before he finally laid down his axe. He was breathing heavily, but he was not finished yet. Six trips he made out to the garden at the back before he had filled the large steel incinerator with that black altar cloth, and all the volumes from the bookshelves. He stood and watched the flames through the kitchen window, laughing insanely to himself. He would win, he felt certain. He would travel to and from the office by bus today!

Mr Theophilus hummed to himself for most of the day. He even smiled, much to the amazement of his colleagues, and when five o'clock finally came round, he left to catch his bus, slightly apprehensive, yet confident that he would avert the fate of which had been warned.

It was precisely 5:45 p.m. when the double-decker bus broke down on the very corner of Barker Street. The engine just seemed to peter out, and for fully ten minutes, the driver and conductor tinkered under the bonnet without success. Then the latter wiped his hands on an oily rag, and shaking his head in despair, he addressed the passengers of the crowded vehicle.

'Sorry folks,' he attempted to grin. 'We'll have to send for the breakdown truck. There'll be another couple of buses along in a few minutes, so if you'd all like to get off, you'll probably be able to get on one of those.'

Mr Theophilus was one of the last to dismount onto the pavement. He had a feeling of portending doom but consoled himself with the thought that the rush hour traffic was too slow moving and congested to be of any danger, anyway. Some children were playing on the pavement, their toys lying everywhere. People stepped carefully around these brightly coloured playthings, and Mr Theophilus followed their example. Suddenly, it seemed as though his feet were moving without the command of his brain. He seemed to be airborne, as though one of his own winged horrors of darkness was claiming him for its Master.

The resounding crack as his head struck the kerbstone caused people to stop in their tracks, and gasp in horror and dismay as blood began to flow from his cracked skull. Meanwhile, the yellow painted toy lorry, upon which he had inadvertently trodden, rolled slowly to the gutter, overturned, and came to rest with its wheels still spinning.

The Immortals

It's strange being in the Fourth Dimension. I've been in it for some time now, and I still feel the same as I did on that very first day, a sort or floating feeling, a sensation of being a spectator to one's own actions. I still look for openings and doorways, in order to go from one room to another, and then I remember, suddenly, that I can pass through walls unhindered. I don't have to bother looking both ways before crossing a jetway. I used to find myself using the subways, until I realised that I could walk through oncoming traffic unhindered, and without any ill effects. It may sound wonderful to anyone who has never experienced it, but after a time it becomes tedious, and then frustrating. I would give anything to get back into the normal run of humanoid life. In fact, I would far rather be a Martian than a 'lost' earthman wandering in a lost world, friendless, and completely cut off from those around me. Naturally, I can converse with humans, and, to all intents and purposes, be accepted as one of then... until they discover my secret. That comes out as soon as I attempt to do anything purely human, such as eating or drinking. My body requires neither food nor sleep. To the casual observer I appear perfectly normal, then a passer-by will bump into me, and go right through me. Bystanders will stand and gasp, and then I'll have to make myself scarce.

But perhaps I'd better go back to the time when it all began. It started on Mars. Where else but Mars could anything like this begin? I'd never given much thought to the F.D. until I met Xavius, that old warhorse of a Martian, a dismissed thereo-scientist, sacked for dealing with matters appertaining to the occult. He hadn't forgotten it, even though it had been almost 25 years ago, way back in 2072. He had just drifted into obscurity as far as the rest of the universe was concerned and concentrated on his own work. He took me back to his place that day we first met. He had obviously taken a liking to me and wanted to explain his project to someone who was prepared to listen.

It was a sight I shall never forget. It consisted of a 6ft, square chamber, the walls of which I could not at first determine clearly, and then I realised that every shade of colour which I had ever seen was represented. There was a transparent door through which an observer on the outside could watch what was happening within. Xavius went into long explanations concerning the complicated panel of dials and switches which rested on a platform outside this unique cubicle.

'I have created immortality,' the ageing Martian concluded, running the six fingers of his blue, scaled and wrinkled hand through his mop of bright yellow hair. It was not hair such as we who had once been accustomed only to mixing with Earthmen knew, but rather several strands of a string-like texture, growing apart from each other. In a younger man they would have been light green, but their present colour was proof that Xavius was a very old man.

'You are immortal, then?' I decided that I had better humour him.

'Alas, no!' he sighed, every regret imaginable being summed up in those two words. 'I am too old, my friend. To go in the machine would kill me. I could not stand the pace and the tension which would have to be generated in order to "send me through". I have only experimented once. It was a success. I want you to meet her very soon.'

'Her!'

'Yes,' he replied. 'A female. The most beautiful girl in the Universe. I have preserved her for all time. She will always be the same. Not a grey hair, nor a wrinkle will she ever know. She will always be Tess, the Earth-girl whom I rescued from the Inter-Planetary Space Police Patrol, so many years ago. She will never grow old!'

'What had she done?'

'Killed a man. He deserved to die, but the laws of this corrupt Universe do not look at it that way. They will have forgotten her by now anyway.'

'Why are you telling me all this?' I asked. 'Showing me something which would be enough to earn you the death sentence - a trip to the Atomic Chamber, from which there is no return!'

'I am telling you,' his voice sunk almost to a whisper, 'because I want you to go into the machine - voluntarily!'

I shrank back in horror and amazement.

'Me!' I gasped, 'No! Not me! Why me?'

'Because,' and he thrust his face closer to mine, 'you are the one man capable of completing the task which I have in mind. And to carry it out you must become immortal. It is the only way!'

'Why me?' I asked again. 'And what is this task you are babbling about?"

'There are two immortal beings in the Universe,' his voice was calm, tolerant, and not a little excited, as I would have expected from a maniac. 'I did not invent this machine. I only borrowed it. It was Tess who brought me the formula, from Earth, where in turn it had been procured from the Powers of Darkness, by one who is more evil than all the worst of Earth and Mars put together. I do not even know the name of this terrible person. All I know is that he, himself, is the other one who has penetrated F.D. Tess wanted to be immortal, and I made her so. I would willingly have destroyed this terrible invention, yet I realised that it was the only means of combating the evil which threatens not only Earth and Mars, but the whole Universe. Mass tragedies are simplicity itself for this power-crazed killer. A vetoship is sabotaged, with a loss of a thousand lives many prominent Earthmen and Martians amongst them - the ruler of Venus, Cratio, was killed with a long distance video-ray, whilst addressing his cabinet. All obstructions are rapidly, ruthlessly, being removed by this murderer in his quest for power. Soon, the entire solar system will be his, unless... unless, my friend, you go into the Fourth Dimension, for only then can his protective armour of invincibility be pierced. He can only be exterminated by one of his own kind. Do you understand me, my friend?'

I nodded, quite incapable of speech.

I cannot fully describe, and do justice to, the sensation of going through! The walls glowed brightly, faded, and then brightened again. They seemed to close in on me, bringing on a feeling of claustrophobia, so that I began screaming. But I need not have worried, for when I opened my eyes again, they had receded. Hardly had I had time to gasp with relief, before the whole place was spinning, faster and faster and still I was hurled from one wall to another, turned upside down, and then, just when I felt that I could stand no more, it came to a standstill, and I sprawled headlong on the floor.

Suddenly, I heard a voice, perhaps from a hidden speaker, or maybe it was telepathy. There was no doubt that it belonged to Xavius.

'You can come out now,' he boomed, in a tone which was full of an authority which I had not noticed previously.

'Well, open up then!' I retorted, thoroughly frightened and shaken by my astounding, yet somehow, exhilarating experience.

'I don't need to,' came the reply. 'Nothing will obstruct your progress now... anywhere!'

He was right. I stretched out my hand towards the door, slowly, gingerly, making contact with it. I began receiving a sensation similar to that of submerging myself in water, yet I was able to breathe perfectly freely. I passed through that metallic structure with ease, no apparent effort being required on my part. Xavius was smiling.

'Well done!' he said. 'Very well done. You are now immortal. You have passed through into the Fourth Dimension. But come, let us not waste time. I want you to meet Tess.'

Tess was one of those girls whose photograph could have adorned the core of every journal published between Earth and Venus without ever once creating a monotony in the eye of the reader. She was ageless. She might have been anything between twenty-five and forty. Her long, blonde hair had not a trace of grey in it, and her complexion was flawless. Her tight-fitting suit was made from a Martian substance called Garnite, showed her figure off to the full. Her deep blue eyes seemed to penetrate into the very depths of my brain, reading my innermost thoughts, and her full red lips parted, showing even rows of flashing white teeth.

'How do you do, Mr. Robinson?' she extended a hand, and I was amazed to find that I could grip it with ease. She was probably the only person in the whole of the Solar System with whom I could shake hands without "passing through", except, of course, for... the nameless one!

'Call me Buck,' I decided on a bold approach.

'O.K. Buck,' she smiled back at me. 'When do we start?'

'We?'

'Tess will be going with you on your mission, Buck,' Xavius cut in. 'She is the only other person who could possibly assist you. Trillions of lives depend on your success!'

I don't remember much about the journey to Earth. We travelled part of the way in a small Riddiocraft, a capsule with just enough capacity to take two adult persons comfortably. Tess piloted it, and I felt somewhat inferior, sitting beside her in the passenger seat We travelled thus, as far as Capitol, an American controlled station, close to the Moon, where we booked in on a Commander IV, a passenger ship with seating accommodation for five thousand people. It was full, mostly with Americans who had been spending their summer vacation at the newly opened Lunar Holiday Camp, a millionaire's paradise, built beneath the surface of the moon. The Australians compared it with Bondi Beach, the Americans with Miami Beach, an example of sheer ingenuity in Twenty-First Century engineering. Everything one could ask for was there, from hydro-controlled surf-bathing to an artificial sun tan. All this, for five thousand dollars per week, including the return to Earth.

The liner hummed along on its way. I felt drowsy, not sleep-wise, because sleep was unnecessary, in fact impossible, in F.D. Perhaps it was just the factor of finally relaxing that made me this way. I looked at Tess, she was engrossed in a magazine which she had purchased back at the station. I could not help but marvel, even after ten years since it was first introduced, at the advantage which plastic pages had over paper. Paper? I didn't remember even seeing a sheet of paper during the last five years or so. Funny old stuff, paper. Still I suppose the lack of timber on Earth, nowadays, made its production almost impossible.

Suddenly everything seemed to explode before me. The whole spacecraft was rent asunder. Debris flew everywhere, and then floated aimlessly. There was not a light to be seen anywhere. Only silence, complete silence. Although I sensed what was happening, I felt no physical pain or reaction. I knew that our enemy had struck again, killing five thousand people in his mad quest to gain complete dictatorship of the Universe. He couldn't harm me, though nor Tess. Tess? Where was Tess?

I felt in pocket for my small emergency light. I was just floating, masses of debris all around me, and at first this was all that the tiny beam of my atomic hand-torch revealed. Limbs, and various parts of the human body were everywhere, and suddenly I felt physically and mentally sick.

'Hi Buck!' I started in alarm as I heard that smooth, honey-coated voice in my ear. Next second Tess drifted into view, grinned, her hair awry, but otherwise completely unharmed, and radiantly lovely.

'Where the hell have you been?' I could not think of anything else to say, and my relief was evident in my voice. I should have known full well that nothing could have happened to her.

'Just drifting around.' Her lilting laugh was grossly out of place amidst this death and destruction, and her light-heartedness infuriated me. 'Seems like our enemy was closer than we thought.'

'We're in trouble now.' I voiced my thoughts. 'We could drift around here until the end of time, and nobody would find us!'

Tess gave a laugh and shook her head. 'Not on this trip, buster. Earth will have had it tele-viewed all the way. They'll have seen the explosion, and, unless I miss my guess, there'll be a rescue capsule on the way right now. All we've got to do is just hang around.'

As always, Tess was right.

It isn't the easiest task in the Universe to find an unknown killer, especially when your only clue is that you're dealing with an immortal being. It does help, though, when you're immortal yourself. The greatest disadvantage, however, was the fact that neither Tess nor I had any kind of official backing. We could not seek the help of any of the universal police forces. They had their own methods of working, and they would have no time for us. In fact, they would regard us as hindrances. They might even dig up Tess's previous record. There was no question about it. We were on our own!

New York was quite a place back in 2097. There was the Upper City and the Lower City. The former was much the same as it was 125 years ago. Many of the original skyscrapers still remained. They will stand until they crumble with age, for historic buildings cannot just be pulled down to make way for progress. However, it is the Lower City which still, to this day, claims the record of one of the finest feats of engineering in the whole Universe. Something on a par with the Lunar Holiday Camp. An elaborate air conditioning and radium-lighting system rivals anything that is to be found above ground. Miles and miles of highways provide extensive means of communications, and, of course, there was the subterrain tunnel to Long Island, which collapsed only last year, killing some ten thousand people. It has never been re-opened since.

But to get back to Lower City, New York. It was here that I decided to start my investigations, simply because it was the only place that I really knew well, and where I had contacts. The scum of the old city, like the rats, preferred to live underground, and thus the Borden area had grown on the outskirts of the new city. The law tolerated it, preferring to have all its vice contained in fifty acres of a space-age slum, rather than spread throughout the rest of the city.

Dakti, the pink-skinned Venusian, was the uncrowned king of Borden, living above his own computerised gambling den.

I had worked for him once before, and now it was to him that I returned. Tess had gone off to San Francisco and I had almost a week to spend on my own. If Dakti knew anything, he would tell me, for he respected me, and, I thought, half feared me.

The gangland boss greeted me like a long lost brother and took me up to his apartment. Everything worked to the push of a button, and within seconds of my arrival I had a plush armchair, a hot meal, and an iced lager at my elbow. Unfortunately, I could use neither!

'So you are with Tess, are you?' he beamed. 'You certainly move in high-society, Buck!'

'She's great!' I replied, feeling my way gingerly, content to let him do all the talking.

'Fabulous is the word,' Dakti answered me. 'I only wish that I was an Earthman. Still, that is only wishful thinking! Now, what did you think of the job on the Lunar Ship? Pretty good, eh! But we must not dwell on past successes. It is the future which matters. Let me show you the schedule of our plans for the next twelve months!'

Minutes later I was looking at a computerised print out of forthcoming "disasters". My heart pounded wildly as I briefly estimated, in my own mind, the millions of deaths which that sheet prophesied, the men of power who would be removed in a twinkling of an eye, as I knew that my search was over. I had not figured on reaching my goal so quickly, but it all added up. Borden Lower City, New York, was the biggest haven of vice and evil in the Universe. Dakti ruled Borden. Dakti was a practiser of the Black Art. Who better to engineer such a diabolically clever scheme and become the First Space-Age Dictator? And only I could stop him!

The Venusian had his back to me now, reaching further information down from a shelf behind where he sat. My hand was in my pocket, and in my palm nestled that small, black, snub-nosed ray-gun which Xavius had given me before I had left Mars. However, it was no ordinary weapon.

'Keep this with you, day and night, my friend,' the old Martian had said. 'It contains a silver-phosphate power-ray the only way in which to exterminate anyone in the Fourth Dimension. Just as a silver bullet killed were-wolves and vampires in olden times, so will this ray kill their modern counterparts. There are two shots in this gun - allowing for one miss only!'

Dakti never knew what hit him. I fired once only and took him in the back. He straightened up, glowed, shrivelled up to a cinder, and then disintegrated. I put the weapon back in my pocket. My task was almost over. All I needed to do now was to examine the files and papers in that room to make sure that disasters already pre-arranged would not go through without the presence of the Master-Mind. I drew up a seat and prepared myself for a few hours of uninterrupted work. It was then that I made the discovery!

The jet-car pulled into the station just as I arrived. It was dead on time, to the exact second. Passenger transport has not failed since the last century, Indeed, it would be almost impossible for modern transport, run by computers, not to keep to time. Eagerly, I scanned the hundred or so passengers who alighted from the gleaming silver car.

Then I saw her. She was as radiantly beautiful as ever. She had bought a new outfit, green and yellow, and for sheer loveliness she was incomparable with any woman I had ever set eyes upon.

'Hallo, Buck.' She ran to greet me, throwing her arms around my neck. 'Any news?'

My lips met hers, and I found them soft, warm, and responsive. My left arm was around her waist, whilst my right hand was cradling the silver-ray gun in my pocket I kissed her again. and then I fired from point-blank range. I stood there, transfixed as she slowly shrivelled up to a blackened cinder, and I was reminded of a book I had once read by a British author named Rider Haggard, about another immortal woman who called herself "Ayesha" or sometimes "She-who-must-be-obeyed". Only this Tess was a far more wicked and terrible proposition. She would not have been content to rule over a lost civilisation. Nothing less than a Universe would have satisfied her. Xavius would never believe me when I told him. He had never once suspected *her*!

As I stood there, mesmerised, I heard a rushing of feet. Cops were everywhere. I made no attempt to escape or resist. It didn't matter anyway. I had destroyed Universal Enemy Number One!

When they gave me life-imprisonment they did not realise what this meant. I just walked out of prison the very next day. Walls cannot hold me! I've spent a thousand years already on Planet 72, a world of outcasts beyond Venus. They call it "Prison Planet". All the dregs of the Universe are to be found here. The law doesn't worry them. It doesn't need to. Nobody ever goes there except to cut themselves off from civilization. They keep on wondering why I don't die. I've seen generations die off in this place, but still I don't appear to be a day older than when I first came here. Xavius must have destroyed his machine, rather than risk it falling into the wrong hands, for I've never heard it mentioned, even on the broadcasts.

Life gets terribly monotonous, day after day, I wish I could die, but I've not even got that to look forward to. I've spent the last few months writing this all down, but they'll only destroy it as the ravings of a madman if they find it. So I'll hide it somewhere. Somebody might find it and read it someday. Perhaps it will be somebody who will pay attention to it and realise how close the Universe was to disaster and dictatorship. As for me, I suppose I'll just go on and on, century after century.

Who knows?

The Big One

'I'm afraid,' Doctor Kemper glanced somewhat furtively at the big raw-boned man who filled the chair on the opposite side of his desk, then averted his gaze. 'The news is not good.'

Out of the corner of his eye the balding doctor looked for a reaction. There was none, the other's expression was impassive. No matter how many times he'd had to convey the worst possible news to a patient over the years it never got any easier.

'Give it me straight, doctor. Let's stop pussy-footing around.'

'All right,' he said with relief that he had not got to embark upon a lengthy rigmarole. 'It's cancer of the most aggressive type. Mostly in the left lung but it has already begun spreading to the right. It's inoperable.'

There was still no reaction from the other, his gimlet ice-blue eyes boring into the doctor.

'How long?'

'Well…'

'How long have I got?'

'Six months, maybe more, maybe less. There's a chance we can slow its progress, but we can't put it in remission.'

'I see.' Carl Strickland scraped back his chair, stood up to his full height. 'Well, thanks for putting me in the picture. I won't take up any more of your time.'

'Wait a minute,' Kemper was somewhat taken aback by the other's cool reception of the worst possible news. 'We can help you, make it easier for you.'

'Make it easier for me to die, eh?' A brief half-smile. 'Drugged up to the eyeballs, lying in a hospital bed. Thanks but no. I'll look after myself, doc.'

'You… you're not going to…' the doctor licked his dry lips.

'No way. I don't plan anything like that, simply that I've got something to do in the time that's left to me.'

'It'd help if you gave up those fags.'

'Bit late for that, isn't it?'

'It might give you an extra few weeks.'

Strickland laughed. 'You know as well as I do what caused this cancer; a glancing blow from a charging Cape buffalo in South Africa a couple of years back. A chest injury that put me in hospital for three weeks. The cancer took time to grow. Now it has. I might've died out there if the bull hadn't had a fatal bullet in its heart. It dropped seconds after it hit me. Otherwise it would probably have gored me to death and I wouldn't be sitting here now listening to your forecast of a slow death. Might've been better but that's how it goes. I got a two-year extension of life for which I'm grateful. So I'll stick with my fags and make the most of every day that's left to me. They're a bonus.'

Doctor Kemper sat staring at the wall for some time after his patient had left. He wondered what it was that Strickland had to do in the months left to him, but the patient was the kind of man whom you didn't put those kinds of questions to.

Out in the street Carl Strickland lit a cigarette, inhaled deeply. A spasm of coughing had passers-by glancing at him in alarm. Right now the first thing he had to do was to phone Konrad Kumer in Mbeya. Time was not on his side.

The small, terraced house was little more than a base for Strickland on those occasions when he was in Britain. The rest of his time was spent abroad in different countries. Hunting. He had the money to pursue such a luxurious lifestyle and he made the most of it. Last year he had hunted polar bears on the ice off Baffin Island and then flown to Switzerland to spend two months in the mountains after mouflon. Then it was back to Africa after the 'Big One', a mighty bull elephant which had eluded hunters for years. It had killed three, a Spaniard and two Americans, all of them with many years of hunting experience under their belts.

The 'Big One', the big prize, trophy tusks for which men had paid tens of thousands of dollars in vain hope. None had succeeded. Not as far as Strickland knew but his priority was to check that out.

Konrad Kumer was the only professional hunter on the Dark Continent who stood any chance of leading a client to success. Unless he had already done so, but there had been no mention of it when Carl had attended the Shot Show in Las Vegas in January. It would have been the talk of the event if somebody had bagged that prized elephant.

Carl Strickland's fingers shook slightly as he picked up the phone. He had already forgotten his visit to Doctor Kemper. He had more pressing matters on his mind.

'Carl, how are you?' The hunter's gravelled tones were somewhat staccato on the line, a grizzled Colonial who had built up an enviable reputation as a PH. Whether you wanted buffalo, lion, leopard or elephant, he got you one. The only prize which had eluded him so far was the Big One. And Kumer wanted *that* as badly as every other hunter.

'I'm fine,' Strickland lied.

'Good. Good. When are you coming back to Mbeya?'

'Depends.'

'On what?'

'A chance at the Big One.'

There was a long silence, then, 'Every hunter wants the Big One. In over ten years none have succeeded. Another was killed a couple of months ago. A German. Highly experienced. The big fella charged him, survived both barrels from a .500/416. The trackers took the German's remains back to camp in a bin liner.'

That's excellent, Strickland thought. *That tusker's still around.*

'He must have half a ton of lead in his thick hide,' Konrad Kumer continued. 'He's tough and he's the most cunning elephant I've ever known. Maybe he'll end up dying a natural death long after you and I have gone.'

'I'd like a go at him, Konrad,' Strickland said. 'Win or lose.'

There was another long silence, almost as if the veteran wasn't prepared to risk it. The toll of hunters was mounting.

'It'll cost you.'

'That's no problem.'

'Thirty thousand dollars for a start, then there's the licence and trophy fee.'

'I'll go for it.'

'I'm free in a couple of weeks, a gap between bookings.'

'Book me in.'

The Toyota pick-up bumped its way along the seemingly never-ending, tortuous track. On either side the scrub plains were burned brown by the relentless heat. Only the coming of the rainy season would save the vegetation. Somehow it always did.

Sam, the tracker, also served as driver, his powerful body hunched over the wheel, constantly glancing from right to left.

'Buffalo,' he pointed. 'There's a good bull with them.'

'It's elephant we're after,' Kumer grunted. 'The Big One.'

'Not to be killed. No bullet will kill him. He kills hunters. He is the god of the Imbezi people. They get very angry with hunters.'

'Then keep clear of them.' A cigarette dangled from the professional hunter's lips, showered ash down his khaki shirt. He was lean of build, his skin wrinkled by a lifetime spent in the heat. It was impossible to judge his age. Strickland put him at somewhere between fifty and seventy. 'We're not looking for trouble.'

'Until we find the Big One.' There was a tremor in the tracker's voice.

'Just find him.' Kumer turned to his client. 'Problem is that dammed elephant spends most of his time on the Lupa Reserve these days. He's cunning, knows he's safe there. We just have to hope that he ventures out and we pick up his spoor,' he said, and shrugged his bony shoulders. 'It's asking a lot, Carl. We might just be lucky. Or unlucky.'

'Show him to me and I'll get him,' Strickland answered, then gave way to a bout of coughing. 'Man or beast, you have to die someday. Sooner, later, depends on your luck.' He wiped his mouth with the back of his hand, noticed a trace of blood. That was how it was these days.

'We'll make camp soon,' Konrad Kumer announced when the sun was sinking low in the sky. 'Start out before daylight. There's a water hole about a mile beyond that clump of trees. Never dries up. Most of the wildlife hereabouts drink there. Could be the big fella fancies quenching his thirst and a bath to go with it. We'll find him tomorrow.'

The early morning was bitterly cold. In an hour or two it would be unbearably hot.

THE BIG ONE

'We'll make as much ground as we can before the heat of the day,' Kumer slung his old Westly Richards double .450 on his shoulder. It was his duty to protect his client, a precise shot in a life-or-death situation. There had been many over the years; he had never failed. He did not relish this safari, and secretly he hoped that the Big One was on the reserve and would stay there.

Three hours later Sam picked up elephant spoor and further on, some droppings. He scooped up a handful of the latter, nodded. 'Fresh,' he announced. 'Sometime during the night. Maybe two, three miles ahead of us. They'll stop to rest soon.'

Konrad Kumer licked his dry lips. 'The Big One amongst them?'

'Maybe, maybe not,' Sam traced an outline of one of the prints with his stick, mentally measuring it. 'That one big. Maybe not big enough.'

Strickland's feet were dragging; he wasn't breathing easily. He turned away each time he coughed, not wanting his companions to see the crimson spots on the hard ground. It was becoming harder than he had thought but he was determined to stick it out. There was nothing else left to him.

By nightfall they had not so much as glimpsed the elephants.

'Travelling fast,' Sam said as they prepared to camp out. 'If they keep going through the night we will never catch up with them. Best to make for the water hole, get there before daylight. It's our only chance.'

Strickland wondered how he was going to make it through the day. His double Holland & Holland .700 seemed to weigh a ton. Nevertheless he gritted his teeth and followed in the wake of Kumer and Sam.

Somehow they made it to the waterhole before dawn. As the sky lightened he saw that it was nothing more than an acre or so of mud. But there was moisture there and at this time of the year that was a scarce commodity out here.

'We'll lie up in those rocks over there.' Sam indicated some scattered boulders, the only vestige of cover. He was edgy. So was Kumer. Strickland trembled for a different reason.

Daylight.

A bunch of warthogs came, wallowed noisily and left. An hour passed and then Sam's ear went down to the ground. Strickland glimpsed the other's expression when he raised himself up, one of momentary fear. Then it passed.

'Elephant,' he whispered, 'coming through the scrub jungle. Just one... *big!*'

Strickland unslung the .700, slid two shells into its breech, closed it with a faint click. God, it was heavy, seemed twice the weight it had been on his last safari. He was sweating heavily.

'I'll tell you when to shoot,' Kumer reminded him. 'And not until. Get it?'

Carl nodded. He would shoot when he judged he had a killing shot within his sights. Kumer didn't figure in his plans.

Now they could hear the elephant approaching, crashing through trees, uprooting some.

Like it's desperate to get to the water.

Then they saw it, a veritable behemoth emerging from cover, trunk and ears swinging.

'It's him!' Carl breathed.

Sam had backed away into the rocks, he was nowhere to be seen. He had found them the beast, his job was done. Nobody hung around when the Big One was close.

Kumer loaded the Westley with trembling fingers. He hoped that he didn't have to fire it. Strickland was a bloody fool to think he could succeed where top hunters had failed. He, too, began to edge away. Carl Strickland was bad medicine in a situation like this, a kind of hoodoo that beckoned death.

The elephant came on at a steady trot, an old bull which had deserted the herd, was living his last days alone. *If* he ever died. The Imbezi believed he was invincible, would live forever. They could be right. Kumer began backing away. Strickland hadn't even noticed, he had eyes only for the Big One.

The elephant halted on the edge of the bog, uplifted its trunk and trumpeted. Almost like it knew the hunter was around and was challenging him. Its mighty tusks gleamed white.

Strickland lifted the heavy double rifle with considerable difficulty, used the rock in front of him as a rest. He took a sighting. Sweat was making his eyes smart, his vision was blurred. His hands were shaking.

The beast turned sideways on. *Perfect*. The hunter's dream, an ear shot where the solid bullet would penetrate, rip into the brain, destroying it instantly.

Strickland pushed the safety catch forward, his forefinger rested on the front trigger. This was it!

He took a deep breath, held it. Squeezed.

The report was deafening, the rifle's recoil throwing his weakened body backwards. He heard the £100,000 gun clattering on the stony ground.

Oh, Jesus!

It was all he could do to crawl to where it lay. He grasped it but he was no longer strong enough to lift it. It was as though his entire strength had evaporated with that shot.

But he didn't need the gun, He had shot the Big One, he couldn't have missed at that distance. It was lying dead by the waterhole. All he had to do was to crawl to where he could see its inert form. He asked nothing else. He had achieved his ambition.

Suddenly the Big One was towering above him, trumpeting its fury. It saw him with eyes that glinted sheer rage. Evil. Another human had dared to try to kill it. Now death was its prerogative.

A huge foot was raised, hovered over Carl Strickland, an executioner's axe poised for a beheading. Gloating, savouring every second.

It came down slowly, seemed to Strickland to be in slow motion, blotting out the sunlight. Darkness. It rested on his chest and stomach; he felt the pressure, his breath being expelled. Bones starting to crack.

He screamed and that was when the Big One went berserk. Its victim's body crushed, squelched; a morass from which arms and legs protruded.

The trunk encircled the human remains, lifted them aloft, swung them high and then dashed them on the jagged rocks. Again and again.

Finally, the Big One lifted the bloody remnants of Carl Strickland to the full extent of its trunk and flung them into the midst of that rocky outcrop.

One final trumpeting and then the elephant turned, ambled back to the waterhole. It took its time bathing in the thick mud, burrowing deep for water with its trunk. Only then did it return whence it had come, a triumphant victor leaving the field of battle.

It was maybe twenty minutes before a hunched, lean figure rose up out of the rocks, wide-brimmed bush hat pushed back on his head, rifle at the ready in case it was needed. It wasn't. Apart from a couple of vultures circling high above there was no sign of life.

Only death.

Kumer saw the bloodied human remains a hundred yards away, fought off the desire to retch. Such 'accidents' were nothing new to him, he had witnessed more than his share over the years. There was no sign of the huge beast. It had wreaked its terrible vengeance and departed, probably back to the safety of the Reserve. Kumer breathed a sigh of relief, lowered the Westly double with trembling hands.

'Sam!' He cupped his hands, shouted. 'It's safe to come out. It's gone.'

The tracker stood up slowly, shaded his eyes and scanned the scrubland as far as the dense patch of jungle. He wouldn't take Kumer's word for it; he had to see for himself. Slowly he began to walk forward, his black features ashen. It might have been the dust. Kumer knew it wasn't.

For some minutes they stood there, not talking. Such happenings as they had witnessed take time to sink in.

'You'd better go and fetch the truck, Sam,' he spoke at last. 'There's some waste bags in the back. We'll need 'em. I'll stop here, keep the vultures off.'

The other turned away, broke into a fast jog like he wanted to be as far away from this place of violent death as possible.

Kumer seated himself on a rock, rifle across his knees. He had a long wait ahead of him but that was fine. He knew that the big feller would not return.

It was strange Strickland missing at that range for the guy was a brilliant shot. He was a sick man, though, that much had been evident since they had left base camp yesterday morning. *If you ask me the guy was dying,* the professional hunter told himself. Maybe the Big One had done him a favour, spared him from weeks of suffering.

At least it was quick.

Greg Mason had been head ranger at the Lupa Reserve for four years. Poaching was the bane of his life, the Imbezi were the worst but at least they only killed to eat. Gangs from further afield were only interested in ivory, left the carcass to rot.

Word reached him that there was a dead elephant by the lake and that tribesmen were already plundering the meat. Doubtless it was the work of the Imbezi and they had poached it.

'It's the Big One,' his informant, who had run five miles to deliver the news, announced.

'In which case the Imbezi would not have killed it because the beast is a god to them.' Mason was already striding to where the battered old Mitsubishi was parked in the compound. 'Probably poachers from one of the other villages. They've nicked the tusks and left the body. I'd better check it out before there's nothing left of it.'

Two hours later he sighted the frenzy of butchering close to some trees by the lakeside, turned the truck off the rough track and bumped his way over ground that became a swamp when the rains came.

There were maybe fifty natives on and around the mighty dead beast. A huge cavern had been hacked out of its side. Machetes and knives were slashing and cutting, joints of flesh thrown out to women who were stowing them in baskets.

Greg Mason braked to a halt, sounded his klaxon. Men froze in their tracks, defiant and guilty stares greeting the newcomer.

'Stop!' Mason jumped down. 'You!' He singled out the tribal chief, arms and legs awash with elephant blood. 'Poaching carries a jail sentence and I guess the cells at Mbeya are going to be very crowded. So you have slain your god, eh?'

'No, boss,' the chief squelched his way out of the beast's belly. 'We no kill. Nor poachers. Elephant die and we find him.'

'Try again, Goma,' Greg shook his head. 'That yarn won't wash with me.'

'It's true,' the chieftain pointed back into the stomach of the elephant. 'You come, see for yourself.'

'I suppose I might as well take a look even if only to prove you a liar,' the ranger picked his way carefully through a morass of slimy intestines.

'See, boss!' Goma was pointing at the morass of lungs that the villagers had cut away, indignant at having his words doubted. 'I tell truth. See for yourself.'

Mason stared; saw a succession of growths on those huge lungs, the size of toy balloons ready to burst. Some had bled profusely before death had stemmed the flow.

He let out a long sigh, nodded an apology to Goma. 'I guess you're right. This animal has been sick for a long time, getting worse day by day. Finally, even his strength gave out so he just lay down and died. Probably in terrible pain. He's survived bullets but he couldn't beat the Big C.'

He turned away, wiped his boots before he got back in the truck. The Big One had killed a hunter only weeks before. Konrad Kumer, the professional hunter, had told the coroner's court that he believed that the guy hadn't had the strength to aim his heavy rifle because he was sick. An autopsy on the remains of the deceased revealed one of the most aggressive types of lung cancer. Now both man and beast were dead, both victims of the Big C. Life could be strange at times, Greg Mason reflected.

And so could death.

The Last Crab

'What a bloody mess!' Stuart Simpson, was small and lean with a lined face which reflected the fifty years over which he had farmed close to this wind-swept tract of Welsh coast. He leant against the side of his parked lorry watching the approaching tractor, it was shovelling up mounds of plastic waste which had been brought ashore by the tide. Shortly his vehicle would be loaded up again and he would make his fourth trip of the day to the landfill site. A dozen or so locals were to be seen gathering up empty drink cans and plastic waste, depositing it in sacks. They were all volunteers who had devoted their time and efforts to support this clean-up operation like himself. The magnitude of the task was awesome.

'Unbelievable!' Andy, his son, in his late twenties and bearing a remarkable likeness to his father, shook his head. 'I hear there's a global, as well as a national, clean-up of the oceans, and there's heavy fines being introduced for litter-bugs. Millions of fish and other sea life are dying from being trapped in plastic waste or eating it.'

'Here's Fred now,' Stuart pointed towards the approaching refuse sweeper. 'Get ready to load up.'

Quarter of an hour later the lorry, with Andy at the wheel and their load secured beneath a large, weighted tarpaulin, was on the road headed for the waste site.

'It bloody stinks,' the younger man wrinkled his nose. 'The sooner we've dumped this lot, the better!'

'You're not kidding, son. And we're doing all this for free like all those folks on the beach scooping up and bagging plastic shit. I guess it wouldn't have gone down too well with the locals if I'd refused. Still, after tomorrow we'll be able to get on with our own work.'

An official at the site recognised them, waved them through to where their load had to be deposited.

'Phew!' Andy held his nose whilst his father released the tarpaulin and pulled the lever which raised the load. The bulk slid, they used forks to free items which had jammed.

'Hey!' Andy peered, ignored the stench. 'Whatever's this, caught up in a torn waste bin liner? It's moving, *it's alive!*'

He prodded the object in question with his fork. The prongs scraped on something hard amidst the shredded material. Something protruded from within, a feeble movement. He tore at the plastic, revealed a shell approximately the size of a young Collie pup, like the one they had back at home.

'Dad… I don't believe this… it's a huge crab! And it's still alive!'

Both men stared in disbelief. The trapped creature was undoubtedly a crustacean, its claws moving feebly, tiny eyes glinting evilly with unmistakable hate for the humans.

'What are we going to do with it?' Andy glanced behind him, saw that the official in a bright yellow jacket had moved away to attend to another arrival.

'We'll take it back home,' Stuart's decision was instant. 'That time years ago, before you were born, huge crabs invaded this shoreline. I think I told you about it. Monsters, they had to call in the army. I reckon this is one of them, a baby. It probably has a mother somewhere out there. Could be worth money to us… if it survives!'

'Where the hell are we going to keep it?'

'That pool you made up behind the house, a flight pond for your duck shooting. The incoming tide flows up that gully, keeps it filled with salt water and it's fenced all round. The bugger wouldn't be able to get out. It doesn't look good, in all probability it will die, but it's worth a chance.'

'I dunno.'

'Lift the trailer back up, Andy, and let's get the hell out of here before that guy over there comes back.'

Reluctantly, the other obeyed. Another of Dad's stupid ideas, he shook his head. If his mother had still been alive she certainly wouldn't have agreed to having a monster crab in that pool so close to the house. Ah, well, time would tell.

THE LAST CRAB

A few minutes later they were back on the road. He thought he could hear a scratching on the boards of the lorry.

On arrival at their small, somewhat dilapidated, cottage he reversed the lorry up to the small gate leading into his pool. The crab had meantime freed itself from the plastic which had covered its entire body, and now clawed feebly at the wooden boards. There was no mistaking the malevolence in its eyes as it regarded its captors.

'We'd better scrape it out with our forks,' Stuart Simpson grunted, 'Chuck it inside the gate and leave it, let it make its own way into the pool... if it can.'

Their captive offered weak resistance as it was dragged down onto the ground. Only when the gate clanged shut did Andy breathe a sigh of relief.

'We'll check on it later.' His father turned away. 'Right now I'm starving. Let's have something to eat. Then we'd better check on the sheep.'

It was turning dusk when father and son went to check on the pool. Reeds fringed the side and the surface was partially covered with algae.

'Where the hell is he?' Stuart grunted when they had completed a circuit of the pond. 'He can't have escaped.'

Andy stared, fixed his gaze on a clump of rushes on the opposite side. Something protruded in their midst. 'He's over there, Dad, it's quite shallow there. Maybe he's died… no, he's just shifted position a fraction. He knows we're here, he's trying to hide.'

'Well, we'll leave him to it,' the farmer pushed the gate open. 'We'll see if he's still around in the morning. Somehow, I think he'll die during the night. God knows how long he was trapped in that plastic sack. Maybe we could polish the shell up. With the history of those crabs it might make decent money at auction.'

The Simpsons always retired to bed around ten o' cock, they needed a good night's sleep as they were generally ready for work soon after daybreak. Tomorrow was market day and they would need to load some ewes into the trailer.

Something awoke Stuart shortly before the alarm clock was due to go off. He lay there listening. A kind of loud clicking noise came from the concrete yard below the bedroom window. A clicking intermingled with a harsh scraping.

What in God's name was going on down there? He leapt out of bed, pulled the curtains wide. Dawn was just breaking, casting a greyish half-light across the farmyard, just enough for him to make out that familiar scene... and something else which was dragging itself across the broken moss-covered stone slabs.

Click - click - clickety - click.

Jesus Christ, it was a crab, almost the size of that cow in the barn opposite which was due to calve next week!

He must be seeing things, his imagination running riot after the previous day. No, it was real enough and now it was slashing at the door with a pincer.

This was crazy, that crab in the pool was only a fraction of the size of this one. An adult crustacean, maybe it had come in search of its offspring, some uncanny sense having guided it to the Simpson's farm.

The sound of splintering wood came from below. It was attacking the door, clearly intent on gaining entry. If the crab in the pool was from its own spawning then why had it not rescued it and returned to the ocean? Perhaps because the latter had died and in some totally unfathomable way the adult was seeking revenge on the humans who had taken it.

Crazy, like a nightmare, but there was no other explanation for the presence of this dawn intruder.

'Dad!'

Even as Andy opened his bedroom door he saw his father emerging from the other side of the landing, partially dressed, his braces hanging down, bootlaces untied.

'What's happening out there?'

'There's a crab out there, not our baby one but a great big bugger trying to smash its way into the house!'

Even as he spoke there came a loud splintering of timber from below and boards crashing on the porch floor.

'Christ, it's nearly indoors, Dad!'

'I'll get the gun.' He turned back towards his bedroom; he always kept his 12-bore in there along with a few cartridges. On more than one occasion over the years he had shot a nocturnal prowling fox from the window. 'That bastard's in for a nasty surprise!'

Within seconds Stuart had returned with his trusty old hammergun which dated back to his grandfather's time. He inserted a couple of heavy buckshot loads, snapped the breech shut.

By this time the remnants of the front door were littering the small hallway and the giant crab was attempting to squeeze through. The open space was too narrow to allow entry so it exerted all of its strength on the surrounds. Stone crumbled, showered. Heavy lumps thudded down onto the floor. Some bounced off the invader's shell, rolled in all directions. The crab seemed impervious to those that struck it.

A thunderous, deafening report shook the interior of the room as Stuart squeezed both triggers simultaneously. Large pellets struck the shell, ricocheted in all directions. A framed family photograph hanging on the wall shattered, fell.

The crab was impregnable to the close range shots, the mighty shell deflecting the pellets.

Stuart reloaded, fired again. Pellets hit their mark but flew in all directions, its small evil face unscathed. It shambled towards the stairway.

Stuart reloaded, fired again. More pellets hit their mark. Broken plaster showered from the ceiling. The crab's lumbering advance was unhindered; it reached the staircase, a claw fastening on the frail bannister. Struts snapped. It started to crawl up the steps.

Up above, Andy had fetched his mobile phone from his bedside table. His fingers trembled as he keyed 999.

There's no bloody signal! he yelled.

Stuart loaded his last two cartridges. Another double shot followed, this time at closer range. The crustacean's features were blood splattered but those eyes were unharmed. The tiny mouth was stretched in an unmistakable snarl of fury.

'Get in the bedroom!' Stuart shouted.

That was when the entire stairway collapsed in a heap, the crab landing amongst the wreckage. Its claws scraped a path to freedom, it crouched amidst the debris, broken woodwork cracking beneath its weight. Those tiny evil eyes were raised, staring at the two humans whose flesh it had been temporarily denied. It was in no hurry. It would wait.

'What're we gonna do?' Andy muttered.

'We'll just have to hope that… that something turns up, somebody sees what's happened. Maybe the postman.'

'We only get the occasional delivery. It could be days. We'll starve up here.'

'Well at least it can't get to us. Maybe it'll give up and go back to the sea. I wonder what's happened to that little'un in the pool?'

'It's probably died overnight. Momma or Poppa came looking for it and wants revenge on the chaps who took it. Let's go back into the bedroom. At least there we don't have to look at that monster. Ugh!'

Bill Stone had been gamekeeper on the small privately owned syndicate shoot adjoining the Simpson farm for the past five years. Short and stocky of build with thinning grey hair he was approaching his seventieth birthday. The job was relatively relaxed and he was hoping to continue for a few more years. Assisted by a youth from the village, he reared a few hundred pheasants.

Poaching had never been a serious problem, just the occasional local 'moocher' in search of a bird or rabbit for the pot. Which was why a sudden burst of shooting just after daylight had him jerking awake.

'Strewth!' he grunted, swung his legs over the side of the bed. 'Who the hell can that be? Maybe it's the Simpson boy putting paid to a fox.'

More shots had him reaching for his clothes. Damn it, he'd better go and check, just in case…

The old Land Rover stuttered into life and he took a short cut across the fields. A few minutes later his headlights focused on the front of the neighbouring cottage, had him gasping in horror at the sight which greeted him. Where the front door had been there was a huge gaping hole as if a bulldozer had rammed it.

He edged the vehicle closer and now the headlights picked out the shambles of the wrecked hallway inside. He gave a gasp of horror and disbelief as he saw what appeared to be a monster crab perched on the wreckage below the collapsed stairs.

He reached for his mobile phone with shaking hands. Whatever was happening in there he needed immediate help. He kept the engine running just in case…

'Police. Can I help you?'

In stuttering, sometimes inarticulate words, he told the officer that something serious was happening at the Simpsons' cottage. 'Some kind of creature that looks like one of those huge crabs from years ago has virtually demolished the place…'

The responding police officer asked for more details but did not seem to regard it as a hoax. Many locals still remembered or had heard from their parents and others involved at the time, of that invasion of Barmouth by giant crabs along with a few more incidents in later years.

'We'll dispatch a unit immediately. In the meantime keep a safe distance from the premises.'

Within twenty minutes a police car was bumping its way along the unsurfaced track which led up to the Simpson's home. They drew up alongside the Land Rover and four Armed Support Unit officers disembarked.

'You must be Mister Stone. What's going on…?'

The officer in charge had no need to wait for a reply for their headlights revealed a huge crab crawling from the cottage doorway. It must have heard their engine and had emerged to investigate.

'Shoot it!' The officer ordered his colleagues. *'Fire at will!'*

Three policemen knelt to steady their aim, each armed with a Heckler & Koch MP5 9mm firearm. These were fitted with 30 – capacity magazines.

A burst of gunfire shattered the stillness of the early morning, a hail of 90 bullets directed at the fearsome creature, all of which found their target. Splinters of shell flew in all directions yet the creature did not slump to the ground. Instead it turned, began to shamble away at a speed which amazed the reloading marksmen.

'Fire!'

Another hail of heavy bullets sprayed the rear of the retreating crustacean, chipping its shell but not slowing its departure.

'Follow it!' Another command, more reloading of weapons.

Bill Stone stumbled in their wake, eager to see the outcome of that concentrated gunfire. Surely that crab would slump down, seriously wounded, its life ended by that final volley from the police armament.

It didn't. If anything its ungainly flight speeded up. Up ahead was the shoreline, a rock strewn beach that met the sand. The tide was fast retreating, leaving in its wake a mass of litter which it had brought ashore.

The crab embarked upon a final flight to safety. Its claws tore into the line of rubbish, plastic items wafted aloft in its wake.

Suddenly it slowed, caught up in a large sheet of thick industrial plastic, its claws entangled yet still capable of movement. Other items of refuse became entwined with it but somehow the creature managed to drag itself as far as the outgoing tide. Waves lapped, and as the depth increased it was lost to view.

'Hold it there,' the commanding officer raised his hand. 'If our bullets haven't finished it off then that mound of plastic will. Right, now we'll head back to the farm and find out how the occupants have fared.'

Stuart and Andy Simpson were standing outside their wrecked home when the rescue party arrived, having lowered themselves to the ground floor with knotted bed linen. Both were clearly quite shaken and related their horrific experience in faltering voices. Almost as an after-thought Stuart mentioned the baby crab in the pool.

'We'd better go and check right away,' was the response. The two farmers and the ageing gamekeeper followed in their wake.

'Blimey, the gate's been forced open!' Stuart announced as they approached.

Up ahead the aluminium 5-barred gate had been wrenched from its posts, lying in a tangled heap. In the soft mud, plain for all to see, were huge claw marks entering and then returning accompanied by smaller ones.

'That big bugger's been and released the youngster,' Andy announced. 'Freed it and then came looking for us. It beggars belief. Hey, see where the tracks part company, the big ones go up to our cottage, the small ones back towards the sea.'

'Where it will undoubtedly become tangled up in that line of plastic rubbish,' the police officer in charge shook his head from side to side. 'Maybe, like its parent, it will make it as far as the tide. But one thing's for certain, both of them are doomed to a slow, horrible death. Terrible as they are, one cannot help feeling sorry for them. The sooner the oceans of the world are cleaned up, the better, but I guess it will be many more years before that happens. The crabs are evil but those that litter and contaminate the seas are just as bad!'

The Taxidermist

Parrish reached the Hanging Wood just as a misty dusk was beginning to creep across the winter landscape. A skimming of snow crunched beneath his booted feet so that he was forced to tread cautiously. Deer have acute hearing and the slightest untoward sound will send them scampering for safety. He could not risk alarming them; he had waited a year for this opportunity.

Parrish was a tall, powerfully built man. The fur lined collar of his thornproof jacket was turned up to protect his aquiline features from the keen wind. Undoubtedly, there would be another sharp frost tonight; heavy snow was forecast for later in the week.

He unsung the .270 rifle from his shoulder, removed the protective cap from a telescopic sight.

Sylvester, the farmer, had phoned this morning to tell him that the hard weather had forced the deer to feed on the remains of the sugar beet crop that adjoined the wood. Bad news for Sylvester, good news for Parrish.

He had left the office early in the hope of a shot, maybe a carcass for the freezer. Only the previous weekend, he and Pattie had eaten the last hunch of the one he'd killed last winter. His adrenaline pumped at the prospect of another beast. Not just the kill, but also the hunt and the anticipation that went with it. His primeval instincts were far from dead.

Leicester Parrish had known this place since he was a boy, when his father had shot in the Hanging Wood and its surrounding fields. Leicester had trailed in his wake, learning his fieldcraft with a puny .410 that had seemed like a cannon at the time. Now the boy was a man, and no mean marksman.

The locals had shunned this place for generations. The wood was so named because Cromwell was reputed to have hanged a hundred royalists here and left their corpses for the crows to feed on. If you were superstitious, on windy nights you reckoned you heard the screams of the victims before the hempen nooses choked their cries.

Parrish wasn't superstitious. He believed that the wood was so named because it hung on the side of a hill. Likewise he scoffed at the stories about the spinney that grew around the quarry three fields below. The Devil's Dressing Room, they called it, where Satan had paused to change into human form upon his return to Earth. In fact, the church which you could see in the distance on a clear day had been built from stone, quarried out of that place; if anything the tiny wood was God's Dressing Room. Parrish had no time for legends or myths; he only accepted facts.

An unearthly roar shattered the frosty stillness, a bestial cry of rage that vibrated the landscape as its echo rolled across to the distant, wooded skyline.

Parrish did not even start; his fingertips, protruding out of the hand-knitted mittens, did not grip the rifle barrel with intensity. He did not stiffen, or glance about him fearfully. Because the cries of wild animals from distant lands were commonplace here; you heard them every evening when darkness fell. And sometimes throughout the nocturnal hours when the moon was full. As it was tonight. But they did not disturb Lester Parrish, for he had long grown accustomed to them.

The small zoo on the outskirts of the village below had long been the subject of local protests. There had been meetings and petitions, but nothing had come of them. Lockhart, the zoo proprietor, was fully licensed to keep dangerous wild animals and there was nothing that the authorities could do to take that privilege away from him. Unless of course, he contravened any of the restrictions imposed upon him.

Last spring a puma had been seen in the locality; a couple of Sylvester's sheep were discovered flayed and eaten. A hunt was organised and the beast was found and shot as it streaked from the cover of the Hanging Wood. Lockhart had vehemently denied that the animal was one of his; it was an escapee from elsewhere whose instincts had bought it here, where the others of its kind roared nightly for their freedom.

Nobody could prove otherwise, but the threat of another escapee was always a very real possibility. Few of the other villagers went outside after dark these days.

The big cat gave voice again. Parrish sighed his annoyance; it might frighten the deer, drive them up to the big wood. No, they were probably used to the noises of jungle animals by now; they sensed that the big feline predators were caged.

Except when one escaped into the countryside.

He leaned up against the tree on the edge of the wood, watched and listened, rifle at the ready. He experienced the uncanny feeling known only to hunters, that tonight he would kill.

Something moved inside the Hanging Wood.

This time Parrish tensed; the rifle was lifted in readiness. The sounds came again; a cracking of a dead twig, the trampling of brittle bracken. Too heavy for a rabbit, even a fox or badger. It had to be a deer.

Just one animal. His trained hearing picked out the footfalls, front and hind legs moving in synchronisation. Coming his way. He estimated that it was twenty metres inside the wood and getting closer with every second.

His temples pounded but his hands remained steady. These were the moments he lived for; the climbing tension; the anticipation of a kill. Everything was right; he was almost invisible against the tree in a deepening dusk, the slight breeze blew towards him. All that remained was a clear sight of his quarry and a steady hand. In his own way, Parrish savoured every second.

The approaching beast halted and in silence Parrish held his breath. It could be no more than ten metres from him, on the very edge of the wood. It was wary, scanning the open ground, alert for possible danger. Had it scented him? No, the wind was in his favour. Had it heard him? Not unless his ears had picked out the hammering of his heart.

He pressed himself back against the tree, lifted the rifle another inch or two. The shot would have to be fast and accurate.

Perhaps the deer had changed its mind, decided to spend the night within the shelter of the wood, browsing low branches. He almost groaned aloud at the thought. A stalk was out of the question; the Hanging Wood was too dark, its floor littered with branches that cracked at every step. You chose your ambush point and waited for your pray to come to you; it was the only way.

A dry bow snapped, dead undergrowth rustled. It was coming; any second its silhouette would be in full view against the starry skyline.

Then he saw it. With the rival stock eased into his shoulder, he looked down the scope, hesitated.

Though it was no deer that he saw against the cross of his lens. It was neither long-legged nor antlered; instead it was powerful and shaggy coated, long muzzle lifted to scent the air, pointed ears erect as they listened.

It was much too large for a fox, three or four times the size of a British vulpine. Too big even for an Alsatian dog. What the hell was it, then?

Down below, the huge feline gave voice again. It was probably Parrish's imagination, but he thought he detected a note of fear in the cry.

The animal ahead of him was starting to turn its head, almost as though it knew that he was there. Parrish's forefinger took trigger pressure, squeezed. The report was sharp and crisp. Flame stabbed from the barrel, the stock kicked lightly against his padded shoulder.

The creature's legs folded beneath its body; its head sagged forward. Then it dropped, did not even roll. It was stone dead before it hit the ground.

The torch beam wavered in his hand. He found himself standing back. So big, so fierce, even in death. Tiny eyes beneath the shaggy hair glinted malevolently; a nerve twitch in a foreleg, and this time he jumped. He loaded another shell just to be on the safe side. The jaws hung wide, saliva strung from the wicked teeth. One bite could sever a limb. Or tear out a throat.

But not this one. He kicked it, jumped clear. It was dead alright. As dead as a .270 bullet could make it, drilled just behind the forelegs so that it ripped through the heart.

Parrish laughed; it sounded cracked and forced. Only then did he realise what species the dead beast was.

It was a fully grown timber wolf.

Of course, it had escaped from the zoo down below. There hadn't been wolves in Britain for at least two centuries, probably more. Just escapees. He found himself turning, swinging the torch in a complete arc, the rifle barrel following it. There was nothing to be seen.

Just a lone wolf that had found a way out of its enclosure. Parrish cradled the rifle in the crook of his arm, licked his lips pensively. Whatever else, the wolf had deprived him of a chance at the deer; they had probably fled the Hanging Wood long before Parrish's arrival. He could return it to Lockheart; there would be no reward for a shot wolf. Or take it to the police. Lockhart would deny ownership; it would have come from another zoo. All of which meant there was nothing in this for Leicester Parrish. He was a rich man but he never did anything that did not offer him some kind of remuneration. That was how he had achieved his status in life.

All that was left was his ego. He pictured the magnificent red stag's head mounted in his hallway. His guests never ceased to admire it, listened awestruck as he recounted that October stalk in the deer forest of Glen Kyle. A 16 pointer.

But others had shot bigger and finer. They hadn't bagged a wolf, though. And Leicester Parrish's thoughts turned to Jonathan...

Jonathan was small and weak looking. His twentieth birthday had preceded Christmas by a week. Three A Levels and two government training schemes had not found him employment. But that which he lacked in size, he compensated for with determination. If he couldn't find a job, he'd create one for himself. His luck changed; he received a business start-up grant and became a taxidermist.

In his youth, he had stuffed rabbits and pigeons for a hobby; mostly his mother consigned his work to the dustbin. Crude efforts, but each one was better than the last. One day he shot a grey squirrel and mounted it. He donated it to the church bazaar, and when he went back the next day there was no sign of it. Mr Shufflebotham, the churchwarden, said that somebody must have brought it if it wasn't lying around amongst the leftovers. It was a heartening thought.

Now taxidermy was for real.

'Well?' Parrish eyed the other's hesitation with some misgivings. 'Can you do it?'

'I'll do it, all right.' Jonathan stroked the wolf's coarse hair. 'It'll cost though, because it's big. Don't know how much until I find out what I'll need in the way of materials.'

'Work it out and make a profit for yourself. A solid plinth, oak, please. I want it to stand in the hallway, jaws wide. Make it look as fierce as you can.' Leicester Parish was unable to conceal his excitement at the prospect of the finished article.

Jonathan shuddered. Mum wouldn't've had that thing in the garden, never mind in the bloomin' house! It was a damn good job they'd gone to visit Dad's brother for a few days. 'Should have it done by the end of the week with a bit of luck.'

'Good lad!' Parrish clapped him on the shoulder. 'I'll call round Saturday afternoon. I want it to be a surprise for my wife.'

Jonathan shuddered again.

'Whatever's the matter with you, Lester?' Pattie Parrish stirred, tugged the duvet back onto her side. 'You've been tossing and turning ever since we came to bed. Something worrying you at the office?'

'No, nothing at all,' he answered with sincerity. 'I always find it difficult to sleep on moonlit nights. I get the urge to be out with the gun, down by the river waiting for moonflighting ducks. Maybe geese if the weather's hard enough.'

'You're mad!' she snapped. 'We're due some new curtains; I'm going to make them up myself, thick and close-fitting so's not a single moonbeam gets through. That way we might get some sleep.'

'You do that.' He lay staring up at the ceiling.

'You didn't manage a deer then?' She was wide awake now. She rarely enquired about his forays with gun and rifle; he seldom told her because he knew that it didn't interest her.

'Didn't see one,' he replied truthfully. 'They must have been feeding elsewhere. Might try again tomorrow.'

He knew that he wouldn't. Because now that his euphoria had died down there was nothing eerie about the Hanging Wood above the village. First a puma, now a wolf. It was like it was an ancient place that beckoned evil, lured creatures that were long gone from this land. Right now he found it hard to scoff at the legends of the Hanging Wood and the Devil's Dressing Room.

Beyond the village an animal howled, its call hanging in the windless atmosphere, slow to disperse. Parrish thought that it sounded like a coyote. It could have been a wolf.

Lester Parrish was an outdoor man, who yearned for the wide open spaces. He told everybody that, as though he needed to justify his executive lifestyle. He would retire at fifty, sell the business and his Midlands home, move North. The Solway Marshes, perhaps. Or the Firth of Tay, where the wild geese wintered and there were stags to be stopped in the mountains.

He was especially restless on sunny winter days. Jackie, his secretary, was anticipating an early finish today; the boss would look in after lunch, tell her to finish what he had dictated in the morning, do some filing and slip-off home, hopefully without the rest of the office staff seeing her go. Lester Parrish had his sneaky benefits even if he didn't pay well.

She had some shopping to do. But she had not expected him to toss everything into the pending basket shortly before midday.

'It's a fabulous day and they're forecasting snow on Thursday.' He pocketed his cigarettes, closed his desk drawers with an air of finality. 'I think I'll make the best of today. Type the letters and do some filing, and don't bother coming back after lunch. If anybody asks, you went to the dentist. With my permission.'

It was as though he had to justify his own absence from the office. Like he felt guilty. Jackie thought that he'd had something on his mind all morning. Maybe he had a row with his missus and was going home to make up. Truthfully, she couldn't care less; this promised a godsend of a half day.

Lester Parrish had not rowed with Patti even if they had bickered during their sleep last night. But he certainly had something on his mind - a dead timber wolf and a rookie taxidermist who was attempting to stuff it. He wondered how Jonathan was progressing. It was early days yet, but he was interested to see how it might be shaping up.

First, though, he would have a leisurely pub lunch at the Chequers. And a couple of stiff whiskies; the police rarely troubled motorists out here. He felt a need to fortify himself. His adrenaline was running again.

The council house had a deserted look about it. Maybe Jonathan had gone to town to buy some materials he needed to stuff and mount the wolf. Or else he was in the shed at the bottom of the garden that served as his workshop. Doing what Lester Parrish was paying him to do.

Parrish hesitated by the gate. Maybe he should leave it for today, come back tomorrow or the day after. It was putting pressure on the youth; he might rush the job, make a hash of it. It wasn't fair to hustle him like he hustled Jackie for letters at the end of the day so that he could sign them and get off home.

Like he was scared to gaze on that dead wolf.

Which was bloody stupid! He pushed the gate open. It creaked loudly. Anybody in the house or the workshop would surely have heard him by now. He waited.

Nobody came.

He walked on down the path, thought about knocking on the side door of the house, changed his mind. There wasn't anybody home, anyway. You could sense it; it exuded an emptiness.

Just like the tatty shed beyond the tuft lawn did. There wasn't anybody in there either. Jonathan had gone to town, taking the midday bus because he didn't drive. He wouldn't be back before four at the earliest; that was when the mid-afternoon bus passed through the village. Pattie used it occasionally, so he knew.

It was a good day to find a cock pheasant on the edge of the big wood. He halted, almost turned and retraced his steps. Another thought, one that brought with it the rush of guilt. Go and have a peep in the workshop, see for yourself. One last glimpse of that dead wolf. Nobody will ever know you've been.

There wasn't any point, he knew what the beast looked like stretched out in death. He wanted to see it standing again, resurrected.

Go on!

The hand that tapped on the warped, second-hand door trembled; the knocking was nervous. Of course, there was no response; he had not expected any.

Take a look inside.

The idea was terrifying now. Like venturing into a mortuary for the first time to view a corpse. It was illogical, the dead couldn't harm you.

The smell hit him like a gust of foul sewer air, a stench of putrescence that caught the back of his throat. He almost retched, turned his head in search of fresh air.

The place was bound to stink, wasn't it? A taxidermist skinned dead creatures, had meat and offal in buckets. All the same, Parrish's flesh goosebumped. An icy trickle began working its way up his spine. He almost turned and ran.

Almost. Except that something held him there. Maybe a spark of curiosity lingered in spite of his fear. Or else he did not trust his legs to take him all the way back to the gate.

Take a look.

He pushed against the door. It scraped back a few inches on the warped floorboards. A sunbeam slanted inside; all he could see was a workbench littered with tools.

He put his shoulder against the door, shoved as hard as he could. It stuck; he pushed again. It gave suddenly, banged back against the wall, nearly threw him. He clutched at the knob, managed to keep his balance.

He hung on, turned and saw. His scream trapped in his throat.

Jonathan lay sprawled on his back, his mouth open in a scream of terror that had died when his throat was torn out. All around him were bloody paw prints, leading off towards the smashed window. Shards of glass littered the floor. There was blood on the cracked sill.

Parish stared in disbelief; Jonathan must have had an accident of some kind. He thought for any logical explanation. Murder! Something had burst in here, killed the fellow and left bloody pad prints before leaping out of the window.

He looked for the wolf's body but discovered it was gone. That was when he finally got his scream out.

ABOUT THE AUTHOR

Guy N. Smith has been a best-selling author for over 40 years. He has written over 70 horror novels since 1975 as well as numerous short stories in the genre.

Find out more at www.guynsmith.com

The Charnel Caves: A Crabs Novel

Horror lurked in the maze of cliff caves where a new generation of giant crabs were breeding.

In 1975 an army of gigantic crabs, the result of an underwater nuclear experiment, attacked the Welsh coastline.

The battle was bloody, many lives were lost until the crustacean invaders were defeated.

Over the ensuing years they turned up in the oceans of the world with further terrible slaughter of humans. Finally, though, it was believed that these monsters from the deep had been eradicated. Only memories of their invasions of land remained with the older inhabitants, tales of their depredations on mankind were whispered but often ridiculed by the modern generations.

Until a few of the survivors returned to the Welsh coast and began breeding secretly in a maze of caverns beneath the cliffs, preparing for a further attack on mankind.

Guy N. Smith Illustrated Bibliography

"The sheer effort and dedication that's gone into creating this unbelievably comprehensive bibliography is breath-taking." – DLS Reviews

The complete(ish) guide to collecting the works of Guy N. Smith.

A journey into collecting the works of prolific author Guy Newman Smith. The book covers all genres of the Great Scribbler's writing and contains over 950 pictures and useful details to assist any would-be collector.

Guy N. Smith Illustrated Bibliography

The author has endeavoured to list and visually represent, through over 950 colour pictures, the vast catalogue of output from Guy N. Smith's 65+ years in print; from the early stories he had published in the Tettenhall Observer and Advertiser paper as a teenager through to the present day. A career that crosses fiction and non-fiction and has covered almost all possible genres along the way, from Self-Sufficiency to Westerns, via Countryside and Glamour magazines of the 70s, all in addition to the numerous horror and thriller titles he is better known for.

Content includes Fiction (all imprints/editions inc. non UK) and Non-Fiction Categories: Horror, Thriller, Countryside and Children's Novels, Omnibus Collections, Chapbooks, Graphic Novels, Anthologies, Fanzines, Booklets, Magazines (70s adult Glamour, Country Sport, Game-keeping, Horror etc.), Periodicals and Newspapers.

The book also contains an original Guy N. Smith short story 'The Beast in the Cage' along with humorous insight into the levels of collecting Guy N. Smith's works in 'The Completist- A Cautionary Tale' by author Shane P.D Agnew.

The Sinister Horror Company is an independent UK publisher of genre fiction. Their mission a simple one – to write, publish and launch innovative and exciting genre fiction.

For further information on the Sinister Horror Company visit:

SinisterHorrorCompany.com
Facebook.com/sinisterhorrorcompany
Twitter @SinisterHC

SINISTERHORRORCOMPANY.COM